the DEVIL TREE II
the Calling

Lisa, Best Wishes. [signature] 2015

KEITH ROMMEL

INSPIRED BY THE LEGEND OF THE DEVIL TREE
IN PORT SAINT LUCIE, FLORIDA

SUNBURY PRESS

Mechanicsburg, PA USA

Published by Sunbury Press, Inc.
105 South Market Street
Mechanicsburg, Pennsylvania 17055

www.sunburypress.com

NOTE: This is a work of fiction. Names, characters, places and incidents are the product of the author's imagination or are used fictitiously, and any resemblance to actual persons, living or dead, business establishments, events or locales is entirely coincidental.

For information about special discounts for bulk purchases, please contact Sunbury Press Orders Dept. at (855) 338-8359 or orders@sunburypress.com.

To request one of our authors for speaking engagements or book signings, please contact Sunbury Press Publicity Dept. at publicity@sunburypress.com.

ISBN: 978-1-62006-652-2 (Hardcover)
ISBN: 978-1-62006-653-9 (Mobipocket)

Library of Congress Control Number: 2015954540

FIRST SUNBURY PRESS EDITION: October 2015

Product of the United States of America
0 1 1 2 3 5 8 13 21 34 55

Set in Bookman Old Style
Designed by Crystal Devine
Cover by Amber Rendon
Edited by Jennifer Melendrez

Continue the Enlightenment!

"I write because I'm addicted to storytelling. What I seek more than another blank page to put down my next idea is a reader who enjoys the stories I tell. Now that's motivation and a reason to keep going." —Keith Rommel

Chapter ④

SACRIFICE

The big oak tree remained firmly planted in the soil and blocked out the moonlight with its thick overhead canopy draped in Spanish moss. It towered there like a sentinel of bad omens with a history it didn't ask for and a reputation it couldn't shake.

A dozen people gathered around, all dressed in long black robes with silk, ropelike belts with tassels and red plastic masks to disguise their faces. Two from the group placed candles around the tree and one followed behind them, lighting the candles. The flicker of candlelight added to the eerie scene that had begun to play out.

Everyone backed away and two others stepped forward. Unlike the others, their masks were white with a bloody teardrop underneath the left eyehole. They brushed away the leaves and acorns that covered the forest floor, sat down on the cool ground, and set a Ouija board between them.

Gentle fingers rested on the planchette, the small, heart-shaped movable indicator, and everyone around remained perfectly quiet. Palpable tension hung in the air as if something wicked shushed everyone with the promise of something terrible to come. The onlookers waited while the two chosen ones who had been called forth spoke to the Ouija board. With that, the ritual had begun.

"We have come here and gathered for you, and we respectfully ask that you give us a sign of your presence," a male voice said, muted by the mask without a mouth hole.

The planchette started to move slowly, without purpose, and the leaders stared at each other.

"Have you been expecting us?" the female said and shook her masked head.

In response to the question, the planchette soon began to push across the board at a rapid pace. It went around in giant circles with such speed that it threatened to fling itself off the board, and the two masked figures struggled to keep their fingertips on the piece.

"We are here for you and wish to do your bidding." The one who spoke looked at the amassed group. "We wish to know your name."

The planchette came to a sudden stop on a letter.

B.

"Yes, thank you for letting us know you are here. There are so many who have come and wish to meet you this night."

The piece darted to the next letter.

A.

"We knew it, didn't we?"

The crowd spoke as one. "We did."

P.

"We want to serve your dark cause and give you sustenance."

H.

The planchette went still. The masked congregation waited.

"Thank you, Baph. I—We are delighted to be in your presence. It is a great honor."

The planchette whipped around the board with a purpose, and the gathered chanted each letter as it was revealed.

F.E.E.D.M.E.

"You need us to feed you right now?"

The planchette moved quickly to the upper left portion of the board and stopped. It landed firmly on the word *Yes.*

The candlelight flickered and dimmed and every other candle blew out. One of the chosen, sitting across the Ouija board from the other, motioned around as if to indicate that there was no wind and no rational explanation as to how that could happen. The tension turned into a feeling of apprehension, and one from the group broke the formation and went to run. The ones to the left and right grabbed the person and kept her in line.

"I don't want to be here," she whispered from behind her mask. "I didn't think it would be like this."

Sounds from the branches above enticed all eyes to look for the source. Fleeting and unwilling to show its features, something that was blacker than the shadows skittered from one branch to another.

"How can we serve you?" one at the board asked.

Again the planchette dashed around the board and the gathered members chanted the letters; the one who wanted to run tried to break free from the people who held her.

S.A.C.R.I.F.I.C.E.

The people standing around fell to their knees and began to chant. The planchette responded to their chant and moved fast again. It made wild swirls and then stopped and started again in fast, erratic motions. The two touching the planchette had a hard time keeping contact with the three-legged wooden object, which had one final order.

N.O.W.

The planchette swirled around again and flew from the board, hitting the one who had tried to flee.

"The decision has been made for us," the female with the white mask said. "The chosen one is already with us."

"No!" the woman said and flailed.

The other white-masked individual stood up and untied the rope with the tasseled end from around his waist. He walked over to the female and wrapped the rope around her neck and pulled. The woman stopped struggling and gurgled.

"Stop being a coward." He let up on the rope.

"Please," she coughed. "My name is Maritza, and I have a family. My friend asked me to come here, and I didn't know it was going to be like this. I believe in God—not what you're doing here."

The female with a white mask exposed a black ivory-handled knife with a serrated blade. Grasping the handle, the figure wielded the dark blade; its owner's mask hid a maniacal smile.

"Well, Maritza, it looks like your being here wasn't by chance. You've been chosen."

"No," Maritza said and shook her head. "Please, take this mask off of me. You can see I'm just a regular girl."

The female with the dagger then lunged forward and plunged the blade into Maritza's neck.

The two who held her let go. The other white-masked leader moved close to Maritza's body and twisted the knife. Blood spurted in thick streams that pumped out of her racing heart. Maritza gasped and made awful sounds as she tried to speak. She tried to use her hands to plug the massive gashes on either side of her neck.

Panting from adrenaline, the attacker dropped the knife and stepped back and watched the regular girl with the family die. Without care, the killer walked around the tree and allowed his hand to caress the rough bark, scarred with ax wounds, burn marks, and a thick cement patch. The blood that covered the hand that was used to stab the dead girl was like a warm glove. The white-masked figure used that hand to smear the sacrificial blood around the massive trunk of the tree.

"We are all here to serve you however you see fit," the figure said and looked into the thick canopy.

Another from the group picked up the knife. "You coward," this figure said and stabbed the dead body over and over again with a contagious anger that excited the gathered group. Hacking at the neck, the cloaked person with a red mask tried to separate the head from the spinal cord but stopped from exhaustion.

Immediately, another came forward and took the knife. Like a wild beast, this masked figure did the same thing, but with an untamed ferocity, until the head separated from the body. Blood had splattered everywhere and the limbs on the body twitched.

"Dig the grave," the person twirling around the tree said.

Retrieving shovels from the surrounding brush, two masked people dug the grave at the base of the tree, careful not to harm the intricate rooting system the tree had developed over a hundred and fifty year time span.

Once the grave was deep enough, the gathered realized that there was no way they could fit the body into the hollowed earth. The size of the hole couldn't be expanded upon because the rooting system was too thick and entangled.

"You and you," the one at the tree said. "Let us see you dismember the body so that it will fit in there. Make sure you remove the face and teeth. I don't want to make it too easy for the police to identify this coward who called herself Maritza."

The two who were called forward bowed in acceptance of their assignment. They knelt beside the body and hacked at the soft flesh, struggling with the bones. When they were done, all that remained was a torso, two separated arms, and broken legs.

"Very good."

The jawless head was placed on the stomach.

"Now," the leader said. "I would like everyone to strip yourselves bare, but masks are to remain on at all times. We must be bound together so that we cannot be divided by law enforcement and their meaningless deals. Remember, if any of you were to leave, become a deserter like this Maritza, then you too will be occupying a shallow grave. Don't serve yourself. Serve what is greater than yourself."

The robes came off, revealing almost an even mixture of both males and females, arousal obvious by the males in the group.

"Now use the blood from the body and paint yourself with it. Cover yourselves from head to toe. Wipe it on the tree, too, as that is your signature, proof of your commitment to Baph and the Devil Tree. Let them know how much we appreciate them and what we would be willing to do for them."

Everyone stuck their hands in the blood and painted themselves. They painted their faces underneath the masks, hands, arms, chests, and legs. The crimson of the blood was lost in the weak remaining candlelight, and they appeared black in the darkness, as if their bodies were still covered with their dark robes. They began to help each other, covering their fellow congregants' backs, making the transformation complete. When they were done, the leader stepped past the tree.

"You two can finish burying the body now. When you are done, you are to join us. The rest of you are to follow me."

Careful where each footfall was placed, they worked their way through the thicket beyond the tree, which seemed impossible to pass. But they shoved the branches out of their way and moved in one steady line.

A small clearing presented itself, and there was a roof overhead. Meshed together by slim trees and the surrounding brush, two twin-sized mattresses awaited them. The group piled onto the mattresses, and in a defiled heap of flesh and extreme passion at what they had just done, they began to slither around with each other and engage in aggressive, almost animalistic sex. They slipped on the blood of the deceased member they were forced to sacrifice as if it were baby oil. The smell of the blood was stimulating, and the idea that they communicated with Baph through the Ouija board was like an aphrodisiac. These dark acts under the canopy of night moved them to celebrate their victory.

Chapter 2

PRISON VISIT

Bill Faulkner sat down in a cold, hard, plastic chair with a harsh steel frame. The room was freezing, and even though the hot Florida sun was baking cars, people, and shelters outside, Bill shivered through the sweat on his brow, nervous about where he was. The strong smell of bleach, encasement of cement walls, and the presence of armed guards was uninviting. How could someone be expected to live in a place like this and find rehabilitation?

It had been a long drive to the Saint Lucie County Jail, and the journey had been filled with personal questions, indecision, and a nagging curiosity. He often thought about turning around and going home, but the feeling conflicted with the sense that he needed to do this for so many reasons.

It had been six months since the Devil Tree incident, and all the stories about what had happened around the tree had gone eerily quiet and were seemingly forgotten. There were no more news reports, newspaper articles, or unruly people being caught and arrested by the tree. Maybe the blemish on the town of Port Saint Lucie was something the people silently chose not to acknowledge and they'd simply buried the unsavory story.

But Bill couldn't get it out of his mind. Night after night, the thought of that tree—the gnarled branches and thick scarred trunk—called out to him. It wanted a visit, and the more he resisted the call the more he thought about it and felt drawn to it.

There were nights he would pace the floor of his small house, his heart driven by a nervous pounding. He would go to the window and look out at the night sky. Some nights, fast-moving clouds and a full moon provided him with natural light to see beyond the C-24 canal sign and to the tree. He would go to the door and grab the handle.

Right there was where he always had his biggest struggle. If he twisted that handle and went out the door, he knew he would be pulled to the tree. He didn't want to know why, but he couldn't get the question out of his head.

So, night after night, he refrained from turning that handle. But his willpower wasn't without its cracks. He had already done something strange to try to quench his desire to return there: he had purchased Jim Perry's house soon after it went on the market. Jim's daughter wanted nothing to do with it, so the county took it and brought it to auction. It was cheap, sold as is, and Bill was the only one interested in purchasing it.

All the furniture had remained behind, as did all of the Perrys' belongings. The place was preserved in a state exactly as it was when Jim murdered his wife, Susan.

It took Bill weeks to clean out the mobile home. He bagged the clothing and dropped it at donation boxes around town. He dragged the things he couldn't give away to the curb and kept very little of what were once the couple's belongings. Jim's worn out recliner remained, and so did the kitchen table. Bill had spent hours scrubbing the bloodstain on the kitchen floor only for it to reappear again a day later. He eventually gave up on it.

The weirdness of staying in the house where Jim had killed his wife because the tree had commanded him to do so still made Bill uncomfortable. But as time went on it was becoming more bearable. He did his best to ignore the strange sounds inside the house that only came at night, and he tried to stay away from the windows and doorknob when he felt the call.

Emerging from his daydream, he stared at a thick piece of glass and watched Jim enter the room with his hands and feet shackled. He looked terrible. Bright purple rings encircled his eyes, and his skin hung loosely on his arms and face. Bruises covered his arms and age spots dotted his skin.

The prison guard undid the shackles that restrained Jim's hands and he sat in the chair and stared at Bill. Bill picked up the phone, and after a long moment of hesitation, Jim did too.

Before Bill spoke, a sudden flutter of nerves beat the inside of his chest and made his hands tremble. Although his hands were still freezing cold, they began to sweat.

"Hello, Mr. Perry, I'm Bill Faulkner."

"I know who you are," Jim said, and a scowl overtook his face. "You're that damn reporter kid. What are you doing here?"

The lines on Jim's face were deep, his hair fully gray now, and his back had a slight hunch to it. Prison life had not been kind to the man.

"I wanted to know what happened that day at your house."

"You know what happened," Jim barked into the phone. "You were there, and whatever you filmed was all over the news and internet. I don't much like you. You and those damn people who tried to glorify something as horrendous as that absolutely sickens me." He shook his head. "I know what I did, and I assure you there was nothing glorious about what happened that day." He held his eyes closed. "Nothing."

"I know that now, and I'm sorry for it," Bill said with a compassionate tone. "But I came here because I need to hear something from you now that you've had some time to think about it."

Jim leaned back in the chair with a smirk.

"Why did you do it?" Bill said.

"Why?" He stared at Bill. "Because she treated me like I was a piece of shit for so damn long I forgot who I was. Something evil played on that. Those bodies I found by that tree were by accident. But it changed me . . . turned me into a monster. Even now as I mention that tree . . ." He shivered and showed Bill his goosed flesh. "At that time I could feel this irritation come over me and I couldn't control it. I couldn't stop thinking about them bodies, what I thought I saw in the tree, and the feeling I had when I was away from it."

Bill nodded and watched Jim's gaze turn inward. His struggle was obvious and real, and anyone who might call this man crazy was mistaken. He was quite sane. As unbelievable as the things he was saying sounded, that tree or something in it did make him do those things.

"What did you see in the tree?"

"I saw the devil himself."

Now Bill's flesh goosed.

"Is the tree still standing?" Jim asked and leaned forward to rest his elbows.

"Yes, it still stands."

"So the rumors are true then. They couldn't cut her down?"

"No," Bill said. "I'm afraid not. They tried to use chainsaws, axes, a two-man saw, and they even tried to burn it. Nothing worked."

Jim tapped the small wooden shelf he rested his elbows on. He shook his head. "That's why I still hear it."

"I want you to know that I don't believe you would have done the things you did if it wasn't for your run-in with that tree."

Jim raised his eyes. "I know there is something afoul with it. The moment I exhumed the bones I released something sinister and it chased me out of there."

Bill nodded to indicate that he was listening.

"I don't mean that in the literal sense. It was more like a feeling or a bad omen. One that told me that I better leave or something bad was going to happen to me." Jim licked his lips. "So I ran away, called the police, and never went back again."

"I know. I saw you talking with the police."

"I'm telling you, whatever is there is pure evil." Jim mused. "I think whatever happened there . . . the evil that played out seeped into that tree. I think the tree gives a little piece of that evil to anyone who crosses its path, and it asks for something in return."

Bill pulled at his chin. "That's very possible. You are not the only one who has been affected by the tree."

"How many others?"

Bill shrugged. "One that I know about."

Jim studied Bill. "It's you. So tell me then," Jim said and moved his face close to the glass. "Have you listened to its call and gone back to the tree at all?"

"No," Bill said and shook his head. "Not since my investigation ended . . . after Schaeffer died."

"So why are you here then?"

"I . . ."

Jim sat back and waited for Bill to answer, but the tortured man on the other side of the glass fell into a long, uncomfortable silence.

"You what, boy?"

Bill looked at him. "I can't stop thinking about it and have this unexplainable need to go there. It's really bad."

"I know exactly what you're saying. But you see, the difference is, the pull that I have can never be satisfied. I can't get back there if I tried. I have these harsh walls and steel bars keeping me from going anywhere. I'm going to spend the rest of my life in here, while I always have to contend with the desire to go back there. I need you to understand that because of what I did I am living in my own private hell every single day."

"I'm sorry. I can't imagine how terrible that must be."

Jim looked at his hands and then showed them to Bill. "I want you to know it wasn't me that did that to my wife."

Bill knew exactly what Jim was saying. He had knocked out a police officer who was at his house because he accused his wife of the murders at the tree. While the officer lay unconscious, Jim attacked his wife and choked her to death right on the kitchen table.

"I bought your house," Bill said, surprising himself that the words came out.

"You what?"

"I'm living in it and have been for the past three months."

Jim sat up straight with eyes as wide as quarters. "You did what?"

"I bought your house. The county took it over and put it up for auction. I know they wanted to demo it, but I showed to bid on the old house and I won—uncontested. I saved the house."

Jim rubbed his eyes. "Now why in the hell would you do something as dumb as that?"

"I don't know," Bill said. "I don't think I had a choice in the matter. I believe I was driven to do that."

"You had a choice back then, as you do now," Jim said and relaxed some by allowing his body to sink back into the seat. "What I'm suggesting you do is to make this right by getting the hell out of there. Let the house rot or burn it down; I don't care. That place is no good and it will bring you bad luck. The curse of that tree and the devil's influence are now inside you. You need to understand that, and to break that bond you need to get as far away from that house and tree as you possibly can. Leave Port Saint Lucie. Leave the state of Florida if you have to."

"I can't."

"You can."

"I've already tried so many times." Bill shook his head and whispered into the phone. "You don't understand. I just can't."

"Well then, I guess I can expect to see you in here with me sometime soon because it's going to drive you mad and have you do something you never thought you were capable of."

"I won't let it get to me."

"That tree is setting you up and you don't even realize it."

"I realize it," Bill said. "That's why I came here. I wanted to look you in the eyes, ask you about what happened, and see what your reaction was going to be like." He licked his lips. "I know for sure you're not crazy. I believe that you getting cursed by the discovery of the bodies and the influence of the Devil Tree is real.

Thank you for taking the time to open up to me, Mr. Perry. I'll come back and visit you soon."

Bill hung up the phone, and he watched Jim do the same.

"Stay away from it," Jim said. And although the glass was too thick to allow the sound of his voice to carry through, Bill could read his lips and see the seriousness behind his gaze easily enough.

Without even thinking it over, Bill knew Jim's warning wasn't enough to keep him away forever. Maybe nothing was enough other than going to the tree and seeing what it wanted. Then maybe that constant feeling of longing would go away.

Chapter ③

LOOKING FOR CLOSURE

Bridget Linne and Elizabeth Brown walked the path that led to the Devil Tree. Birds sang and a gentle breeze rocked the treetops and masked the fact that something so terrifying had happened to them near here, it had taken them a half a year to try to face their fears.

The girls paused in their progress and looked around. Even though everything felt safe and the daylight offered them security in what they were about to do, they knew they were going to come face to face with the thing that gave them nightmares. This tree was where the serial killer Gerard John Schaeffer had intended on torturing and killing them.

They held hands and tried to keep each other from trembling. Taking a step and then another on the path toward the tree, they continued their slow approach, talking to one another in whispers of reassurances.

Elizabeth grasped a bouquet of flowers in her hand, not realizing she was snapping the stems. The two moved at a slow pace with eyes as big as silver dollars.

"My heart is pounding so hard it feels like it's going to come out of my chest," Bridget said.

"Mine too," Elizabeth said.

"We need to this," Bridget said.

"Yes, we do."

"I hope we're almost there."

They continued on the path and soon saw the tree. Massive and old, it merely looked like an unassuming ancient tree, but they knew it had a thirst for blood—and at one time it was their blood it wanted.

Last time their fates had been entwined with the tree's dark desires they were at the hands of a killer; now they had come to give the tree an offering of peace. The peace was only partially intended for the tree though—it was also meant as a gesture for the people who had died there.

Before they made the trip out to Oak Hammock Park and made the journey past the C-24 canal sign, Elizabeth and Bridget had bought the bouquet of flowers to put at the base of the tree as a symbol of love and beauty. Maybe that gesture would enable them to put this whole thing with their captor and the Devil Tree behind them for good.

They needed to move on, and in this moment they needed each other for comfort and encouragement. Once they set the flowers down, Bridget wanted to say a prayer for the people who had lost their lives there. She hoped that if those people were trapped there, her prayer could help release them.

They both knew they were lucky to have escaped the killer's wrath and often talked about it late into the night and wrote down how they felt. The idea of keeping a journal to help them cope with the traumatizing event was Elizabeth's idea—an idea Bridget loved and found great meaning in.

Making journal entries during difficult days had helped to ease the mental anguish of their ordeal. It was a great way for them to collectively cope with the ups and downs of trauma and tragedy. Over the past several months the girls had begun to readjust to everyday life and returned to work. They saw less of each other but made it a priority that they speak at least once a week. Today was one of those things they promised to do, and now they were almost there, ready to leave the things that happened in the past there and look forward into a bright future.

"Even though the sight of this thing scares me, I'm glad you pushed us to follow through with our promise to each other to do this," Bridget said.

"I'm beginning to think it wasn't such a good idea after all," Elizabeth said and stopped. Her body shook.

Bridget tugged Elizabeth onward. "Come on, we can do this." They approached the tree, and as they rounded the hulking trunk, a heaping mound of freshly turned earth just about the size of a burial site made them gasp.

Elizabeth dropped the bouquet and Bridget jumped back. The two made a fast retreat and stopped when they were a safe distance away.

"What the hell did we just see?" Elizabeth said. Her pupils were pinpoints.

"I don't know," Bridget said.

"I know what it looked like to me," Elizabeth said.

"I do too."

"Please tell me that's not another burial site."

"I . . . I don't think I can," Bridget said.

"But he died!" Elizabeth said and collapsed to her knees. "He hanged himself at the tree! When is this going to end?"

"He didn't do this . . . he couldn't have," Bridget said and took out her cell phone and dialed 911.

"Yes he did!" Elizabeth shouted. "It's his legacy! People just won't let that die with him, will they?"

"I don't know."

"Why do they need to torment us? Don't they know we've been through enough?" Elizabeth rocked back and forth on her knees and pulled at her hair. "I just want him to go away! I want my life back."

"Hello," Bridget said into the phone. "My name is Bridget Linne, and I'm at Oak Hammock Park. I think there's been another killing at the Devil Tree."

Bridget nodded her head. "Yes, that's what I said, at the Devil Tree." She nodded again. "OK, we'll wait, but we're going out to the parking lot. We don't want to be near that tree."

Bridget hung up the phone and helped Elizabeth to her feet.

"Come on," she said. "Let's get out of here."

The women made a hasty retreat. Each one sobbed, Elizabeth more so than Bridget. They whispered frantically on their trek back to the parking lot, trying to come to terms with what they just saw and having to face the idea that there was still evil lurking about, killing in Schaeffer's name. And knowing that made them feel very uneasy.

"Maybe it was an animal," Bridget said.

"That was a big burial site to be an animal."

"I don't know. Maybe some crazy person did a ritual or something . . . maybe they sacrificed a lot of animals. I don't want to believe that is a person in there."

Elizabeth looked at her friend through red eyes. "Neither do I. I don't think I can handle that."

Chapter 4

BLOG POST

Bill Faulkner plopped down in his chair, his mind tired from thinking about everything Jim had to say. He pulled himself close to his computer desk and turned on the computer. While he waited for it to boot, nerves made him crack his knuckles and shift around in his seat.

After the murderer behind the original Devil Tree case had been exposed and had died at the tree by hanging himself, Bill swore he would never revisit this topic again. But that was proving to be an impossible promise to keep. Here he sat, knowing he was logging on to make a blog post. It would alert thousands of people, making them aware of his reentry into the forum that had remained wordless for over six months. Knowing this was going to happen went against his own word to never bother with the tree or anything that had to do with it ever again. And yet he couldn't force himself to get up and walk away.

Was it the tree that had motivated him to buy Jim Perry's house and go visit him in prison? He didn't want to believe it was true, but the events were too coincidental. And as absurd as that question might sound even to him, there was no question he was inserting himself into something that had affected him and many others profoundly.

Every day he thought about it though: No matter where he went and what he did, the Devil Tree and the things that happened there occupied his mind to the point of not being able to focus. That's when he bought Jim's house. He figured that maybe if he was closer to the location of one of the events the pull would ease up some. It hadn't, however, and that was exactly the thing that Jim warned him about.

The computer blinked to life and Bill logged onto the internet. He clicked on the shortcut on the browser toolbar and logged into his WordPress page.

"I can't believe I'm doing this," he said and sighed. He sat back in his seat and felt a smidgen of doubt, and he desperately tried to latch onto that. He was done with journalism and had looked into any job that would pay the bills. He'd found a good place to work but he was never really there. The pay was good, but the stress and hours of being in retail while being bothered by the pull of needing to go to the tree was the perfect mix for him to fail.

So he quit and thought about the tree all day long. Things were progressing for the worse, and though it felt out of his control, it didn't go unnoticed. He had gone to see Jim. Now he stared at the computer screen and decided that if this is what he was going to do again, he would have to find a balance between allowing obsession to take control and treating this as a regular job.

Bill realized that it was important not to get sucked into this to the point where it took every moment of his day and only intensified his fixation. That was going to be his biggest challenge, and he had yet to formulate a plan to distract himself.

"This thing has me bad, and I don't understand why," he said. He shoved his fingers through his hair and sighed. His hands hovered over the keyboard, and soon his fingers began hitting the keys at a frantic pace of about 65 words a minute.

The Devil Tree
The Man the Tree Commanded

I never thought in a million years I would do what I did today, let alone make another post concerning the Devil Tree. If I'm to be honest with you all, I have to tell you that I've had a difficult time keeping the tree from my mind, and I've tried desperately to occupy myself with other things, but to no avail. I fear it has attached itself to me as it has many others before me.

Today I visited Jim Perry. For those of you who don't know or remember, he is the man who originally found the bodies at the Devil Tree. After his accidental discovery, his life quickly spiraled out of control.

I remember seeing him in his driveway moments after he attacked a sheriff's deputy so he could kill his wife. He had gone into a blind rage that motivated him to strangle her to death. He used his bare hands and crushed her windpipe. The crime was senseless and driven by evil.

At that time, Jim was on record as saying it was the tree that had commanded him to do that. He warned others to stay away from it because he claimed it would instill the same evil desires in them. I listened to that warning but not without a hankering to satisfy the pull to return to the tree, which is so hard to explain.

When I left the Port Saint Lucie prison earlier today, I had just seen a man who had aged dramatically in six months. He spoke of his own pull to return to the tree and his frustration that bars and brick walls prevented him from doing so. He spoke of a longing, which I compare to a hunger, that can never be sated.

While I spoke to him and looked into his eyes, I didn't get the feeling that he was nuts by any stretch of the imagination. He is as normal as you and I.

He revealed to me that he had a terrible marriage and became worn down by life. When he came upon the tree, he discovered something . . . he couldn't possibly understand what it was and what it would do to him.

Affected by the bodies he found, paranoia set in and he began to suspect his wife had committed the crimes to set him up. The combination of believing she was the killer and being on the receiving end of decades of mistreatment was the perfect combination to feed on his fears and push him over the edge, causing him to kill.

I remember him looking at his own bare hands—the weapon used to kill his wife—and telling me it wasn't him that did it.

I understood what Jim was trying to tell me. Yes, it was his physical presence but not his normal submissive behavior, his personality, or his free will. He believed then as he does now that the tree is what commanded him to do the things he did. Had Schaeffer's evil seeped into that tree and allowed it to call out to people and directly influence them?

That's a question I can't answer.

Before I left the prison, Jim warned me that the tree was sucking me back into its service. That's where I hope he is a little crazy and a lot wrong.

But that pull I speak of is so hard to explain and ignore. Just like hearing Jim's statement that he believes he saw the actual devil himself at the Devil Tree.

Bill Faulkner – staff writer

Bill posted the entry and shivered. Somehow and some way he had been sucked right back into reporting about that damn tree, and admitting to that realization broke his will to fight it.

Just then, his police scanner went off. It was an emergency call to Oak Hammock Park . . . Bill closed his eyes, inhaled, and smiled: the tree was calling out to him.

He grabbed his voice recorder and cell phone, which he used as a camera and video recorder, and hurried out the door.

There was no time to consider if the events that were unfolding were coincidence, or if he was truly, finally in service of the Devil Tree.

Chapter ⑤

AGAIN

Officers Abernathy and Breck were the first on the scene. They left their squad cars with lights on close to the C-24 canal entrance. It was a statement to the community and to the reporters that local authorities were there and, like last time, they wanted everyone out and not to cross the C-24 canal sign.

"I don't like this place," Abernathy said. "I never liked this place." He looked at the flow of the canal and then to the forest. "Having to be here now brings back bad memories I'd rather forget."

"I can't say I blame you," Breck said. He was handling the yellow Police Line tape. "I think we would all like to put what Schaeffer did behind us. You, me, every man and woman on the force, and the entire damn town for that matter."

"He put a blemish on the precinct and with it a fear of who might be wearing this uniform. It's going to take years to wash away what he did."

"I know it," Breck said as he tied the yellow tape off on a tree across from the C-24 canal entrance fence post. "Did you ever notice how this magical yellow line does wonders . . . like those plastic stick things at the supermarket. You know, the ones you put between your groceries and someone else's?"

"Yeah," Abernathy said and laughed.

"It's like it's an electric fence."

"Thanks for the distraction from all this. I needed that. Reminds me though: I think my wife runs that yellow tape down the middle of our bed every night."

"Oh, troubles for the little guy in your pocket?"

"I've had no interest either, to be honest," Abernathy said and turned away. Ever since Schaeffer fooled him, he hadn't felt the same about himself or the people around him. Trust was no longer his strong suit, and nightmares were a part of his sleeping pattern.

Lately it seemed his knack for discovering obscure details had been clouded by his own personal doubt. He had worked side by side with a serial killer and didn't even suspect it. How could he miss that?

Because of his inability to see what Schaeffer was doing right under his nose, that maniac had gone on to try to kill two more people. Thankfully, they escaped. Abernathy was relieved not to have their deaths on his conscience.

"Here comes the cavalry," Breck said.

"Just like last time," Abernathy said and adjusted his bulletproof vest. "Are the girls secure?"

"Secure in the back of my squad car. Hopefully everyone will be so fixated on what's going on here they won't notice them."

"We'll get them out of here as soon as possible," Abernathy said. "I doubt they want to be anywhere near here."

The mobile forensics team, cadaver dogs, the dive team, and a handful of officers arrived and immediately began to go to work by the orders of the new captain. His name was Brian Moore, and he was the youngest to ever reach the rank of captain on the Treasure Coast.

"So what do we have?" a K9 officer named Jensen Blackmore asked. He had full control over his 80 pound German Shepherd by a tight chain leash and a police vest wrapped around his furry body. The dog stared down the canal path and whimpered with his tongue hanging out of the side of his mouth.

Officer Blackmore reached down and patted him on the side. "Good boy. We're going to get to work in just a second."

"I hate to say it, but two young ladies may have found another body underneath the tree."

"*The* tree?"

Abernathy nodded his head. "Yes, that tree again."

"Damn. Did they say what they were doing here?" Blackmore said.

"Not yet," Breck said. "Being who these girls are, however, now is not the time."

Blackmore nodded, his confusion obvious.

"They're in the back seat of my patrol car," Breck said and motioned to where he was parked. From where they were standing they could see the shadows of the two young women in the back seat of the running vehicle. The ladies were hidden fairly well by the window tint, so Blackmore moved around to try to get a better look.

"Oh," Blackmore said, breaking his gaze on the car. "Who are they?"

"They're the girls who escaped from Schaeffer. We're waiting for Captain Moore to let us know what he'd like us to do with them before we transport them. The one girl in that car was the one responsible for beating the crap out of Schaeffer, which gave them the opportunity to escape."

"She's bad ass. But you've got to be shitting me. I mean imagine the chances." Officer Blackmore lifted his chin toward the patrol car. "How are they doing?"

"Not good. As you can imagine, they're shaken up pretty bad," Abernathy said.

Blackmore shook his head and didn't look at the patrol car again. "Those two have been through enough. I just wonder what they were doing here. It doesn't seem like a place they'd like to be." He pursed his lips and looked off into the distance. "This is going to make people crazy about this damn tree again. I'll catch up with you guys later."

Blackmore allowed his dog to lead the way. He followed the path that would lead him to the Devil Tree. The dog pulled him along, its nose close to the ground.

"That conversation didn't end too soon. Here come the vampires," Breck said and nodded beyond the yellow tape.

Reporters' vans pulled into the parking lot, all with their respective emblems advertising their channels on the side of the vehicle. Satellite dishes sat atop the vans and the doors swung open upon arrival. Each van spewed two people: a camera operator and someone with a microphone, fixing their clothes and looking around. In less than a minute, the media sharks descended upon the scene.

Bill Faulkner had arrived more quietly. The distraction the larger media outlets provided allowed him to approach the yellow tape without even being detected. He looked over his shoulder and then at Abernathy.

"Let me guess," Bill said. "There's another body at the tree?"

"It appears that way," Abernathy said. "It's unconfirmed as of now because it's just a dirt mound the size of a small grave. Forensics is going to have to see what's there. If there's a body, this crap is going to start all over again and we're going to have to try to figure out how the body got there, who it is, and why they were there."

"Where is this small grave?" Bill asked.

"It's underneath the tree. They placed it about three feet away from the trunk," Breck said.

"The sight of it just being there is disturbing and brings up things from the past, you know?" Abernathy said. "What is it with this tree?"

"I don't know." Bill shook his head. "I wish I knew."

"I'm surprised to see you here. I thought you quit reporting after everything that happened with the Schaeffer case."

"Yeah, I did too."

"Is the tree calling you back into service?"

"It sure looks that way for all of us, doesn't it?" Bill looked back again as the reporters started their charge toward the yellow tape. "Can you tell me who the two women in the back of your car are?"

Abernathy kicked at the dirt. "You don't miss much, do you?"

Bill shrugged. "It's my job not to miss much."

"Yeah," Abernathy said. "Mine too." He fell into silence.

"You know we can't say anything right now, Bill. We have to protect their identities until we can interview them and get a statement. You know if their names got out to the media that juggernaut would steamroll them. Let them be and don't mention them to anyone right now."

"Fair enough," Bill said. "We've already had this dance the first go round, and I know how it works."

"I appreciate that," Abernathy said. "When the time comes, I'll fill you in on some of the details."

"I know you will, and I appreciate that. You are a man of your word."

"You too."

"Hey," Breck said. "Make way for the big guys unless you want to get crushed by the lunatic mob willing to sell their souls for the little bit of information Abernathy just gave you."

"I don't worry about them," Bill said and moved aside. It was a spectacle to see the charging media descend upon the yellow tape and take a few steps into it, stretching it just to get that much closer. Microphones, cameras, and shouting reporters turned the whole thing into a circus.

"Back away and calm down," Abernathy said and took a step toward the yellow tape.

"You know we're not going to answer any of your questions," Breck said. "So why don't you put your microphones down and lower your cameras. The crime scene is still fresh, and forensics just got here. They're assessing what was found and what might have happened here."

"Does it have anything to do with the Devil Tree?" a reporter managed to shout audibly over the melee.

An instant quiet inserted itself between the reporters and the police. Breck looked at Abernathy, and Abernathy reached for a camera lens and pushed it away.

"Fucking vultures! Now why are you asking questions like that?" He shook his head. "Are you trying to get people in the town all upset over the superstition surrounding this tree when you don't have any facts? You're a bunch of idiots."

"I would hardly call it a superstition if murders keep happening by the tree," the reporter rebutted. "And don't touch my camera or my cameraman."

"I'll do a whole hell of a lot more than that if you so much as step a toe past this yellow line," Abernathy said as Breck squeezed his shoulder and turned him away. "You people push and push until someone's life gets destroyed. Learn discretion, you soulless vultures," Abernathy shouted over his shoulder.

"The people have a right to know what's going on in their community!"

Abernathy spun on his heel. "You're speculating that another murder has occurred. Do you know something I don't? I'd be more than happy to take you downtown to question you."

"You know I had nothing to do with whatever is going on here, and your scare tactics aren't going to keep me from doing my job. I'll continue to ask the tough questions that need to be answered. If you won't answer them then I'll find someone else willing to talk."

"No one is going to talk to you."

"Maybe they should have someone standing guard who doesn't have such a hot temper. Remember the *serve* part of your job, Officer."

"Let me reiterate this," Abernathy said. "How about you and your bloodsucker friends take a few steps back? You're stretching the yellow tape, pushing yourselves into our space. If any of you continue to do that—and I mean any of you—I'm going to arrest you for impeding on an active crime scene."

Breck approached the wall of reporters and camera operators with his arms spread. He encouraged them back and they responded by backing up. Abernathy stared at them, obviously hating that they were present right now and trying to dig up something that should be left alone.

Bill used the distraction the news reporters were making to remove his voice-activated electronic recorder from his pocket. He turned it on and was pleased to see the bright red light turn on once he pressed the record button.

He knew he would never know who was in the squad car by questioning the police just the same way he knew he wouldn't know what was going on underneath that tree. So he had to improvise and think outside the box.

With a quick flick of his wrist, he tossed the recorder into the heavy brush beyond the yellow tape. He aimed for the spot where Abernathy had pulled him to the side some months back when he was asking questions about Jim Perry when he first found the body underneath the tree.

Later tonight he would come back in the cover of darkness to retrieve the recorder and see what information he could capture.

"Take it easy, Officers," Bill said and nodded at his fellow reporters. "Don't let them get to you."

Bill stuffed his hands into his jeans pockets and turned around and walked away knowing he still had it. His plan was ingenious, and he hoped it would pay off.

Chapter 6

MAKING THE ROUNDS

Darkness blanketed Oak Hammock Park and attempted to cover all the secrets and horrible deeds in an eerie shroud. Mist had settled in and around the forest, lending an eerie feel to the already mysterious area.

The yellow police line remained in place and flapped in the breeze. A single police car was parked just outside the C-24 entrance, and a lone officer named Danny Lenza was assigned to patrol and keep the crime scene secure.

Lenza exited his vehicle and turned on his four D-cell Mag Light flashlight, and the bright beam slashed through the night fog with ease. Hitting the trees with his beam, he moved the light to the path underneath his feet and then back to the woodsy area.

He wasn't thrilled he had been assigned this detail alone. There had been chatter around the precinct for months that something unexplainable was going on at the Devil Tree. After Schaeffer did what he did, it was strongly believed that the tree and the surrounding area were undeniably haunted.

Pushing that to the back of his mind, Officer Lenza went on this walk every fifteen minutes to make sure local thugs and Devil

Tree enthusiasts stayed away. The night had been quiet, and the moon remained hidden by fast-moving clouds, leaving Lenza to rely heavily on his flashlight.

As he walked the path beyond the C-24 canal sign he couldn't help but think of the stories. He squeezed his flashlight and hoped it didn't fail him. If he were to find himself encased in darkness deep inside these woods, he might not find his way out of the maze of trees until dawn. The thought, like the others that busied his mind, was irrational and unpleasant. He shook his head to clear the thoughts. He had a radio; he could call in, and the other officers who were on duty would come get him.

He wiped sweat from his brow and turned left on the path that would lead him to the Devil Tree. As he approached it, he shined his light into the thick canopy and swore he saw something moving from one branch to another.

"That was a squirrel," he said aloud to himself and shivered.

He searched the treetop some more and didn't see any sign of the animal. A heavy, repelling feeling almost chased him away, but he remained by the scarred tree with the thick trunk and massive crooked branches draped with Spanish moss. The soil under his feet was loose from the now empty grave forensics had meticulously opened and then filled in after they exhumed the butchered body of an unknown female.

"It was a ritualistic killing," Captain Moore had told him.

"Don't you think you should have someone there with me?" Lenza said.

"I don't think you're going to see anything more than the bottom of your coffee cup," Captain Moore said. "It should be an easy night for you. If you run into any trouble, don't confront it. Radio it in and wait for backup."

Lenza nodded.

"I'm not kidding," Captain Moore said. "If some kook decides to visit the tree knowing there was a ton of activity around here today, he's probably not all there. All that has happened here should keep anyone with half a brain away."

"OK," Lenza had said but now regretted doing so. He had been making his rounds and radioing them in like clockwork, spending most of the time trying to fend off an indescribable unpleasant feeling rather than any tangible threat.

Resisting his continuing need to flee and give in to the legend, he inspected the thicket around the tree but didn't see anything out of the ordinary.

The path continued past the tree, and Lenza shined his light down there. Broken beer bottles littered the ground. He decided to take a walk down the path, using his flashlight like a light saber. When he got about 20 yards away from the tree, he saw that the path thinned. Looking left and right, to his surprise he saw cinderblock frames from what looked like a very old building. Moss and fallen trees concealed the structure well, but Lenza's watchful eye did a better job of identifying them.

He searched onward, and it seemed the farther he went in, the more of these old, weather-beaten skeletal frames he found. This was the first time he had ever taken notice of the remnants; he would bring it up to his fellow officers to see if they had noticed them, too. Someone had to know their origin.

After counting about eight different structure frames, he snapped some pictures using his cell phone and then turned around and returned to the tree. Thumbing his radio button, he leaned his head toward his shoulder and said, "Lenza here. Everything is still quiet."

"Ten-four," dispatch responded.

"This is one creepy place," he radioed dispatch.

"Never seen it and never will," the soft voice of a woman responded. "I've heard some bad things about the place."

"Like what?" Lenza said and checked what was behind him. There was nothing but a vivid imagination and a fear that had followed him since the moment he left his squad car.

"Come on, Lenza, they call it the Devil Tree. Do you really need further explanation?"

"No. But I want to thank you for giving me the creeps even more than I already have them. I'm standing right next to the damn thing as we speak."

Lenza moved his flashlight around. He hated the way the undergrowth cast weird shadows he couldn't make sense of. It added to the scare factor. He shivered and turned on his heel and hurried out of the forest and onto the C-24 path. He didn't care that he ran away because he knew no one was looking. He glanced over his shoulder one last time and was glad he was putting some distance between himself and the tree for another fifteen minutes.

When he got into the squad car, he locked the doors and glanced in his rearview mirror for good measure. Curious as to what he had come across past the tree, he turned on his phone and opened his photos.

One after the other, he stared at captured the remnants of cinderblock walls that had crumbled over time. Corrugated steel lay rusted, which Lenza was sure was part of the roof.

He opened the text application and messaged his wife: *I came across these old ruins while on patrol tonight. I know how much you like looking at things like this. Give the baby a kiss for me.*

He attached the pictures and sent the message.

Chapter 7

THE STRANGE HOUSE

Bill stared at the ceiling in the dark bedroom. His mind raced with thoughts of the tree, the killing he just knew had taken place there again, and the voice recorder he'd tossed into the underbrush. Maybe he would be lucky enough to have captured a conversation between some of the officers giving away the details they worked so hard to keep private.

In his mind, he tried to figure out if his tactic was dishonest or not. He needed answers he would never get otherwise. The decision to dump the recorder was creative; a good reporter would think his way around any and all obstacles to get the story. He considered himself to be a truth seeker, and using what little tools he had at his disposal to obtain that truth did not make him dishonest, he rationalized.

A vehicle with its headlights on passed his house, and the light arced across the ceiling and disappeared only to encase him in darkness again. He closed his eyes and could picture himself looking up the fat trunk of the ancient tree. The gnarled limbs gave an impression of some sort of deformity—like they were twisted because they belonged to the devil. The thought of what might live in that tree and the bodies that were hanged on those branches made him shift uncomfortably in the cot he laid in. Then there was the possibility that the bodies that were buried by the base of the tree were indeed feeding the tree, and in turn, their essence becoming a part of the tree.

He hated how dark his thoughts were becoming. To think he was going to get up any minute now and walk through that forest to try to locate his recorder unnerved him. His heart worked the inside of his ribcage, and he could feel a tremble in all of his limbs. Maybe he should leave the recorder and just forget about this. Walk away as Jim had suggested. Pack a bag and drive out of town.

Panic made his heart pound faster and harder. He sat up quickly and swung his feet onto the floor and tried to calm down. He had to think things through a little more before he rushed out into the night and journeyed through a blackened forest he promised himself he would stay away from. He also had to consider the possibility of heeding Jim's warning while he had the chance.

"You planted the recorder," he argued with himself. "If you want the story, you're going to have to put your big boy pants on and get the damn thing before the police find it. Brave the forest, face your fears, and come home safe and sound. That is just a regular tree where bad people go to do bad things."

He sighed.

"Maybe it would be easier if I just got a bag together and rode out of town. Stayed someplace new and tried to settle in there. Leave this madness behind."

His shoulders fell forward and he shook his head. A deep sigh filled the room and the words about leaving echoed in his head—

they didn't sound right. Turning his back on a story where he could make a difference wasn't an option.

"Into the dreaded forest I go," he said and dressed in a matter of minutes. He tested a pen flashlight and stuffed it into his pocket.

As Bill was getting ready, it didn't escape his notice that the mobile home was exceptionally quiet tonight. It didn't creak or groan, crack or crunch like it normally did. Often he would be lying in bed and would hear the sounds the house would make. Sometimes the noises were so deliberate, he thought someone was in the house with him at first. He soon came to the conclusion that Jim's wife's restless soul was roaming about. Maybe she was unsettled and was trying to figure out what happened to her. The sudden trauma of her homicide was quick and brutal, and it very well may have trapped her here.

"You're quiet tonight, Susan," Bill said, and his nerves began to calm. He walked into the kitchen and looked at the area where Jim had strangled her to death. He could see the blood stain on the floor even without the lights on. That blood belonged to Officer Abernathy. "Are you upset because I went to see Jim today?"

Bill listened, but everything was perfectly quiet.

"Are you angry at me for going to see him?"

Bill listened again, and the house remained quiet.

"I suppose a part of me regrets buying this place. If I would've known you were still here I would have let them knock it down so you could move on. But I didn't know you were here, and this house, like the tree, has an allure to it. The violence that absorbed into the walls and floor from the trauma that was suffered here gives me a feeling like the one I get when I'm called to that tree."

He shook his head. "I don't know why I would want to be around that—or a haunted house."

Bill laughed. Here he was talking to a house where he believed a dead woman roamed. Every bit of his conversation was genuine and meant for Susan if she were really there.

Maybe he was slowly going crazy and like Jim said he would break and do something to someone that he would forever regret.

"I want to tell you that I went to see Jim today because I wanted to know why he did what he did to you. I got answers from him that I don't think you're going to like so I won't tell you. Maybe one day you can find your peace and move on. For now I'm going to be leaving, but I'm only going to be gone for a short time. Do me a favor and watch over the house for me. Keep the bad out and you stay in."

Bill exited the house, jogged to the nearby Oak Hammock Park, and used the cover of darkness to advance toward his goal of retrieving his recorder.

Certain there would be a strong police presence, he would have to be extra careful and elusive to claim his recorder.

Chapter ⑧

CEMENT PATCH

The dark figure was dressed in a black robe with a hood pulled over its head, watching the police officer and the beam of his flashlight leave before moving forward.

In the figure's right hand was a large chisel, which he raised as he approached the tree. Using a free hand to feel around the tree and locate the edges of the cement patch, the shrouded figure inserted the chisel into divots and began to pry away at the hardened cement that had solidified onto the tree with an incredible amount of strength. It remained vigilant in keeping whatever it covered from ever being exposed again.

After working the chisel all around, the cement chipped away and fell to the ground in small bits. The massive slab seemed unmovable. Using his hands to try to locate a larger breach to slide the chisel into, the shrouded figure found one toward the middle of the slab's very left side where it failed to wrap around the bark.

Inserting the chisel into that hole, he leaned his entire body into it, jerking back and forth to crack the patch. Finally it gave way and allowed an opening large enough to get the entire tool into the hole. With three hefty shoves, the cement cracked into a half dozen chunks and fell to the ground with a heavy thump.

The man placed his hand on the tree where the cement patch once was and could feel the engravings that were left behind by Schaeffer. It was a glorious moment to be the first to see his work and a bigger honor to be able to touch it. The power that coursed through his hands was incredible.

Kneeling, the cloaked man bowed down and began to pray something unholy.

Chapter ⑨

RETRIEVAL

From a darkened clump of dense foliage somewhere near the entrance of the park, Bill watched the patrol car sitting in front of the C-24 gate.

The officer was easy to see, and although Bill didn't know him, regardless of his own reputation in helping to solve the Schaeffer murders, he knew his presence wouldn't be welcomed.

The last thing the cops wanted to deal with was reporters. Well, that and family disputes. The status of a reporter was about even with a used car salesman with a giant trust-me smile. Knowing that, he decided it was best to use the back entrance.

Taking to the streets, he took the long walk around the darkened neighborhood and jogged for short distances to cut down on the time.

Once he reached the slated wooden sign welcoming visitors to Oak Hammock Park, he hopped the rusty locked fence entangled with flora. Beyond the barrier, thick forestry stood in his way. This entrance had been installed but was never used and the forest had claimed it as its own.

Grabbing the penlight was the smartest thing he'd done so far tonight. Navigating through the treacherous terrain—where thorn bushes, spiderwebs, poison ivy, snakes, wild boar, bobcats, and other wild animals posed a constant danger—was made slightly more bearable with the assistance of the penlight. The concentrated beam of light at least gave him a chance to avoid the treacherous things that awaited one wrong move.

Careful with each footfall so as not to draw the attention of anyone or anything, he continued to move at a slow and steady pace. He headed on a course that he was certain would take him directly to the Devil Tree.

Although that wasn't his desired destination, it was a massive landmark he could use to locate the area where he had tossed the recorder. And while he was there he would have a look at the tree and the grounds. It would be interesting to see what the forensics team had done around the tree.

After about fifteen grueling minutes of making his way through a thicket that grabbed at his clothing and hacked at his skin, he found the tree. As he approached it, a sense of foreboding entered his body and encouraged his feet to carry him away from there as fast as they could.

But he needed to see.

Scattered rubble at his feet was identifiable as the cement slab he knew covered the occult engravings Schaeffer had left behind. Bill thought at first that the forensics team might have done this, or maybe the killers who dug the grave at his feet had done it, but something told him this just happened.

His mini penlight beam cut through the night and he looked all around frantically, sweeping over everything so fast that even if something were there, he wouldn't be able to see it.

The sound of sticks breaking iced his blood, and he tried to get a sense of which direction the sound had come from. He steadied his light. His feet might as well have been made of cement as the sound rumbled toward him. Bill didn't spot the bobcat fresh on the trail of game until the last second when it sprinted past him.

Breathing a sigh of relief, he shined his penlight on the occult engravings. A haphazard pentagram was etched into the wood and so was the word BAPH. He remembered seeing this engraving six months ago, and looking at it now made him feel uneasy like something big and awful had come back to Port Saint Lucie.

Someone had purposely exposed Schaeffer's work—and recently. This was an obvious message; one he heard loud and clear. As he walked away, he shined the light at the ground. The loose earth that had been someone's grave looked like it was no bigger than the size of a child. He thought of Jim Perry and what it must have been like to uncover those bones. It had to be similar to the way the women who found this new scene felt.

Whatever was going on here, between the ritualistic killings and repeating scenarios, there seemed to be a clear involvement of a cult. Bill was doubtful that it was simply random fanatics celebrating the evil that was done here because the killing had elevated to a level beyond that of the average murderer. He didn't need to listen to a recording to know that.

Bill moved on and stuck to cover as he advanced toward the location of his recorder. He used the light sparingly and had to hide behind a thick cluster of trees when a flashlight beam slashed the night and brushed over him. Pressing himself flat against a tree, he tried to become one with the forest.

The patrolling officer moved onward, oblivious to Bill's proximity. Once the officer was far enough away, Bill moved quickly. He knelt before the patch of foliage he had thrown his recorder into and used his penlight to search. He raked his fingers through the rotting leaves and moved quickly. Sure the officer would be circling back soon, Bill guessed he had three to five minutes at best.

"Come on, where are you?" Bill muttered. If he found the recorder in time, he could sneak under the yellow tape and exit the park through the front instead of having to fight his way through the thicket and take the long way out.

After several frantic moments of searching, he found his recorder, brushed the debris off of it, and stuffed it in his pocket. He ran out of the park, mindful not to go in front of the cruiser in case it had a dash camera rolling.

Once he was out on the streets he slowed to a walk and removed the recorder and started to listen to the hysteria of the local media asking the officers for answers to their question. He forwarded the recording and could clearly hear Abernathy and Breck grumbling their distaste for the media and the way they came off as hounds.

Up the walkway and into the mobile home stained with a violent past, Bill sat on his cot and continued to listen closely to the recordings. Fast forwarding and listening to what was being said in two minute intervals, Bill realized that the things that had been captured were too distant for him to hear. Sometimes there were just too many people talking at once and everything was jumbled.

Disappointed by the results, he forwarded some more and listened for another minute in hopes that he had by chance caught the Holy Grail he was looking for. Still, there was just more jumbled chatter and long pockets of silence. Footsteps could be heard regularly, and it seemed that as brilliant as his idea was, it wouldn't reveal anything to him other than how chaotic things can be behind the scenes.

He forwarded the recording again, but this time he went much deeper into the time line. When he pressed play, as clear as day he could hear Captain Moore talking to Abernathy.

"The two women Schaeffer abducted six months ago came to the tree with a bouquet of flowers," Abernathy said.

"Ah, shit," the captain called out. Shuffling sounds filled the microphone. "It's not as if they haven't been through enough with him driving them out here at gunpoint."

"Being a police officer and dressed like a damn woman to boot," Abernathy said.

"Sheesh."

"What do you want me to do with them?"

"Take them in. Have the shrink talk to them and see if they're all right."

"Anything else?"

Silence between the captain and Abernathy was filled by the background noise of people coming and going.

"No. Not right now," the captain said. "Let them be. What more can they tell us other than what we see here?"

"I don't think anything."

"I don't either."

"Why don't you go ahead and get them out of this park. I want you to personally take them to our headquarters. This is not a good place for you or them. Get going."

"Thank you, Captain."

Footsteps could be heard moving away from the recorder.

"Abernathy?"

The footsteps stopped.

"Yes, Captain?"

"How are you?"

"I'm fine."

"I really mean what I'm asking you, and I'm looking for an honest answer. How are you?"

"I'm good, Cap."

The footsteps faded into the distance.

Bill smiled and shut off the recorder. The Holy Grail sat in the palm of his hands. This was a reporter's dream come true, and none of those high-paid people could even touch what he was able to do this day. He placed the recorder on the nightstand next to his bed.

He was fighting excitement and exhaustion at the same time. His need to hear all the details on that recorder could wait until morning, but he yearned to hear them now.

His day had been full and his night had been run mostly on adrenaline. He decided to leave the recorder where it was and close his eyes and try to forget about everything—even the noises that were coming out of the unoccupied kitchen.

Once he woke up, he would go over the recording thoroughly and take notes on everything that was said. Somewhere in there was a victim's name—it had to be. Then he would follow up on the best leads and see if they brought him any closer to figuring this thing out.

Chapter 40

CONTACT

Danny Lenza looked at his watch. He had pushed this perimeter check out by five minutes, dreading having to walk the path to the tree again. It was like the Green Mile only worse, if that were possible.

He exited the comfort of his patrol car and adjusted his utility belt. The sound of the leather creaked, and so did his aching lower back from sitting so much in one position. The pictures he had taken of the ruins were truly remarkable, and he studied them again since sending them to his wife. The abandoned structures had to be fifty years or older.

Officer Lenza clicked the button on the flashlight, and the all-too-familiar canal and treeline lit up as he walked past the C-24 canal fence for the eighth time tonight. The fog had blown through and the humidity had finally let up.

Apprehension beat the inside of his chest the moment he thought about leaving his squad car; now the thing inside was working him over.

As he walked the path and meandered onto the high grass, he realized that no matter how many trips he made to the Devil Tree, it never got easier. A sense of dread surrounded him like death was walking arm in arm with him. It was a silly feeling he hated to admit even to himself. It was like he was a scared kid; but putting aside his shame, something just wasn't right with this area. People didn't belong here.

"I hate this damn tree, that stupid canal, and I can't wait until this assignment is over," he said aloud. "I hope they give it to someone else tomorrow."

Pressing the button on his radio, he leaned his head toward his shoulder.

"Ten-twenty, I'm walking the grounds again."

"Ten-four," dispatch responded. "Eyes up, Lenza. Nothing is ever routine."

Lenza smiled. "Ten-four, dispatch," he said. Just like that, all of the bad feelings that were colliding into each other inside his head and chest slowed down and he focused on observing. Survival was his mission.

Lenza moved his light into the thicket to make sure he was alone and then back onto the path he walked. Rocks and roots were a tripping hazard, and he was being careful not to hurt himself. The night had been perfectly quiet with the exception of having to deal with his own fears and doubts that rattled around inside his head and always seemed to get the better of him.

As he continued his approach to the tree, this moment proved to be no different than the previous seven times. Being in battle with something unseen was ten times worse than dealing with a perpetrator that stood five feet away and chose to run. When things like that happened, there wasn't much time to think about anything.

Turning onto the path that led to the Devil Tree, the uneasiness that entered Lenza's body became heavier, slowing his pace and demanding his focus. His neck tingled, and a warm sensation shot through his body. This was the first time this had happened, and he didn't have an explanation as to why it had happened at all. He continued to work the flashlight beam all around and study things a bit more carefully.

As he approached the tree, his beam swept over a shape he almost missed standing next to the massive trunk, and he centered his light on what he saw. There, blended into the night was a person dressed in a black robe with a hood on and they had their back to him.

Lenza drew his sidearm and aimed it at the person. "Show me your hands and turn around slowly," he shouted.

The shrouded person remained perfectly still.

Officer Lenza took a few cautious steps forward. "I said to put your fucking hands on top of your head and turn around slowly and face me."

The person raised their hands high in the air and turned and faced Officer Lenza. The figure wore a red mask that had horns coming out by the forehead.

"What the fuck?" Lenza said and stumbled backward. He clenched the flashlight between his head and shoulder. His finger hugged the trigger and his left hand cupped his right hand, wrapping around the butt and bottom of the gun, keeping it perfectly still.

"Don't make any sudden movements or I'll shoot you. Do you understand me?"

The cloaked person just stood there, hands in the air. Officer Lenza was able to key his radio by taking one hand off the gun. "Ten-twenty-five, I'm using a zero as we speak."

"Ten-four."

"Ten-twenty-four, dispatch."

"Ten-four. En route."

"Dispatch, Ten-twenty-four."

"Ten-four."

Lenza moved both hands onto his weapon again, and the flashlight shifted slightly, illuminating the area around the perp. His eyes remained focused and he trained the handgun on the center of the person's chest. He was a good shot—one of the best in the academy. He just had to keep his head and maintain control over the situation at all times.

"Turn back around, and I want you to get on your knees. Cross your legs and put your hands behind your back."

The cloaked person followed the instructions exactly. Lenza moved slowly, keeping his aim steady and his attention on high alert. He moved the flashlight to his hand so he could scan the shrubbery quickly before he moved toward the person shrouded in black.

Once he got to the perpetrator, he holstered his weapon and grabbed an arm and pulled it behind the stranger's back. He reached for the other arm, and as he was swinging it down, he heard rustling in the tree above.

Everything in the moment that followed seemed unreal: The kneeling figure, the tree, and Lenza's fear and understanding of the dangers his job put him in somehow all came together in an instant. He looked up to see what made that sound but was only given a second before something dressed in black leapt out of the tree and fell on top of him.

The force of the blow was massive, and Lenza fell to the ground. The wind was knocked out of his lungs and he lost his hold on the stranger in black.

As fast as he was jumped, his wits came slamming back into his head as he struggled to gather air. He watched faceless people dressed in black emerge from deep within the surrounding vegetation and descend upon him.

They were on him in a matter of seconds; before he could react, they had disarmed him. Outnumbered and unable to fight back, Officer Lenza wanted to beg and plead for his life, to tell them all why they should let him go, but they punched and kicked him. He curled into the fetal position to help thwart the blows, and his vest did a good job of reducing the impact to his back and ribs. But there were so many of them and they all seemed to be fueled by an obsession and a rage Lenza couldn't understand.

They landed bone-crushing blows that made him dizzy and unable to catch his breath. But he had to try something because they were trying to kill him.

"Please," he gasped. "I have a wife and a young child at home."

They continued to punch and kick, leaving no part of his body untouched.

"I don't want to die this way," Lenza said, still curled into a ball. "Not here. Not like this."

They kept attacking.

"Why don't you cowards put one person in at a time so I can beat the hell out of them? At least make the fight fair."

His arms were pulled away from his face by two people, and a third punched him in the mouth multiple times. Lenza's lips went numb as they swelled in a matter of seconds and his teeth broke loose in his mouth.

Chapter 00

OVERTIRED

Bill turned on the lamp that sat on top of the computer table. He woke up the computer he'd placed in sleep mode and pulled the chair out. With a mind full of so much information and even more questions that he couldn't possibly sleep, he plopped down in the chair and felt the sting of exhaustion make his tired eyes water.

"I'm no freelancer," he said aloud to the room. "I'm a servant to this tree and the things that it reaps."

The cursor blinked at him, and he was slow to respond. His fingers hovered over the keyboard; his thoughts were disorganized and fleeting. He focused on the reason he couldn't sleep and suddenly found his fingers tapping away as his thoughts sped up and showed no signs of slowing down.

The Devil Tree
Something I Did

No matter how hard I try, I am unable to sleep. I've been in bed for hours and I've been unable to quiet my mind. So here I sit at my computer, hoping to deliver a cohesive message.

I know the reason I'm so restless. I've been wrestling with emotions that have me equally unsettled and contemplative. I did something today that blurs the line of ethics as a reporter, and the strong sense of conviction that I have is not taking it easy on my conscience. I suppose my punishment is lack of sleep.

I'd like to inform you that I've come across some very sensitive information about the events that took place at the Devil Tree earlier in the day. If you didn't hear, there was a call made by someone who believed they found another body at the tree.

The idea that someone found another body out there at all is disturbing in itself, but the person who found it makes it even creepier. I'm talking top-of-the-line bizarre stuff here, people.

I've already decided I'm going to withhold the person's name because I don't want to be responsible for turning anyone's life upside down. The media is a rabid pit bull, and the person I'd name would merely be its newest chew toy.

So if you are the person who was involved with today's events, rest assured: I may have crossed an ethical line to obtain the information about you, but I'm not going to share it. That would be unfair and wrong to do.

Another affliction that ails me is that I have enough of my own problems when it comes to that tree. It seems to suck in people it has unfinished business with. I know I am one of those persons, and I believe I am headed for something most unpleasant. I might as well resist it as much as I can.

If you are reading this and asking yourself why I'm telling you these things, it is twofold. One, I don't want to be responsible for bringing negative attention to anyone. Second, I'm trying to clear a guilty conscience.

The feeling I get being around that tree and the general area is unpleasant. I wish I had a better word to describe it. Evil? Possessed? Haunted? Creepy? Like a nightmare? Yes, those things, too. But simply put, it is a repelling feeling. Ask anyone who has been around that tree and you will find a commonality that is impossible to ignore. Remember before when I said it has an allure? That's what I'm talking about.

Imagine you have a feeling of being pulled to this tree, and no matter how much you resist it, you somehow find yourself tangled up in the next mess that comes along. I no longer believe in coincidence. In fact, I think it is the tree, and whether the devil is there or not, something dark and sinister is, and somehow I've been encouraged to write this passage.

Funny how the word 'encouraged' has the word 'raged' in it. My inability to escape the tree's pull puts me in that place.

Getting back to my guilty conscience.

When dealing with dark things, isn't one supposed to bend the rules a bit to try to get the upper hand? I'd like to think so, but I'm not sure, and my mind won't leave me alone about it.

Sleeping pills topped off with a Xanax will be the only end to this for the night. Until I can find some understanding of the things that I have unearthed, I can only hint at what I know. Remember this before you leave my website: something evil still plagues Port Saint Lucie's Devil Tree, and people are going to endure horrific things because of it. Stay away from it. I mean it. Stay away. I can't explain it, but I can feel the omen deep in my bones.

Bill Faulkner – weary and sleep-deprived staff writer

Chapter 02

OFFERING

Officer Lenza was bleeding badly and still unable to fight back. The people in black cloaks stripped him of his utility belt and they tore at his shirt, ripping it to shreds. They pulled off his shoes and pants like a pack of wolves devouring their prey, peeling the layers off him to get what was beneath the clothes—and soon the skin.

Naked on the cool ground beneath the Devil Tree, he tried to crawl away. He clawed at the soil and rotting leaves, the surface roots and fallen acorns slicing into his exposed flesh. Then he reached the grave and his fingers sank into the soft soil, and for a moment he could relax; the soft dirt was like a pillow.

"Please," he said through fat bloody lips and broken teeth. "I have a wife and a young child at home."

Maybe if he were to stall long enough, backup would arrive in time to help him.

"That's too bad, Mr. Police Man," someone said. Their voices were muffled by the masks they wore.

"We've come to give the tree what Schaeffer intended to give before someone stopped him. I believe he was someone just like you."

"My wife," Lenza whimpered. "My child . . ."

"That is such a sad story. I only wish they were here with you so we could use them as sacrifices, too. But there is no time to stop us from what we need to do. If I were to thank you for your sacrifice, would that make you feel better?"

"No, please . . ." Lenza said again and continued to dig stiff fingers into the ground. As he moved onto the harder ground he could feel his fingernails and flesh ripping away. He groaned and struggled with every effort, but knowing his hands and skin were the least of his problems, he continued on.

Although he moved at a snail's pace, he was determined to try to buy himself enough time so that his brothers in arms could save him. They always looked out for one another, protected each other no matter what it took, and he knew they were coming.

"Give me my knife," the person who taunted Lenza said to another cloaked figure. Acorns crunched underfoot as someone came forward. Lenza looked up and saw the second stranger hold up a black knife with a vicious curved blade and serrated teeth at the end. The officer whimpered as the black ivory handle with a goat's head engraved into it was presented to the person with the murderous intent.

"Prepare the noose," someone he couldn't see said, and he watched through eyes that were beginning to close from the swelling. Things were blurry and distorted and he battled to regain his focus. He saw his tormentor take control of the dagger and raise it to the tree, presenting it like an offering. All he could see was a mass of people dressed in black moving closer to the tree and bowing.

"We do this for you," the cloaked person said. "Let this man's fear, his blood, and his life help sustain and satisfy you like Maritza's did."

"No, please," Lenza said, and his head fell to the ground. He breathed so hard that he blew the rotting leaves away and sucked in a mouthful of dirt. He was out of time, and he knew it. Where was the cavalry?

With a slow and calculating movement, the cloaked individual pressed the knife into Lenza's flesh between his shoulder blades and sunk it in slowly, turning the knife so it slid in between his ribs.

An explosion of pain ripped through Lenza, and he screamed and kicked and felt an awful pressure behind his eyes. With an expenditure of the last of his energy he tried to call out to his wife and child, but a knee pressed down on his back and kept him from being able to take in another breath. Everything hurt, even the breeze that caressed his flesh and the blackness that began to overtake him.

With full body weight pressed down on the officer, the tormentor and killer sunk the knife all the way in until the man twitched. The skin, muscle, and bones were tough and required full strength to get the blade deep enough to penetrate vital organs.

Once the knife was fully inside, the twist of the handle was to ensure the victim would bleed out faster on the inside.

The strategy worked because soon the body stopped moving completely and a chorus of hushed thanks came from the congregation. The dagger was ripped from the body and people moved forward and turned him over.

Someone used their own knife to cut open the abdomen and the crowd reached into the carcass and pulled out the warm slimy insides. Some of the people bit into the innards and began chewing on them, groaning in satisfaction.

"Drag him to the noose," the killer said.

The frenzy halted and they placed the head into the noose and cinched the rope around the neck.

"Now pick him up! Let's finish this and give the tree what it wants!"

Several people pulled on the rope and lifted the dead man high into the tree. Blood spilled onto the ground and the dead officer's entrails hung out of his belly. A mound of organs was discarded on the ground where the attack had begun.

Some members began to hang the organs from the tree.

The killer dropped the knife to the ground, walked over to the officer's clothing, found the radio, held the button, and breathed into the microphone. "Your officer is down and your backup is too late. His death was glorious and he gave his life for the tree. You need to know there will be more. Plenty more. Come and find me and stop me if you can."

Chapter ~~1~~ 3

THE VOICE OF EVIL

Bill listened to his police scanner, and having heard the officer's report about the trespasser at the park at the Devil Tree, he sat in contemplation. Although he was tempted to run to the park to try to get a firsthand look at the events that were unfolding, he didn't want to go against his own ominous warning from his latest blog post.

He also knew that if he was the first to report on the events, he would be able to give his increasing audience an inside look at how serious this Devil Tree danger was. The decision to stay or go weighed heavily on him. The story wasn't worth a thing compared to a man's life and the torment he must have experienced when he discovered someone at the tree. The distress could be heard in his voice. That call from the officer banged around inside Bill's head and showed no signs of stopping.

He remained seated and decided he wouldn't go out there. Whatever was going on out there wasn't this horrific scene unfolding in Bill's mind. It was more than likely a curious kid having a look around. But the shiver that rocked his body told him it was probably something worse. It was something to be feared, just like Jim had said.

Go.

He sat back in his chair and listened. Had he just heard the voice of Susan trying to guide him in his decision making? Odd sounds that moved throughout the house followed, and he wondered if he really had the company of a ghost or if he was slowly going crazy. What he experienced was certainly unexplainable, and every time he went to check on what he was hearing, the house would suddenly go quiet. Left to his own imagination on what was really happening inside the house where a husband murdered his wife, there was still a measure of uncertainty that plagued him. It crept in through dreams and wild imagination.

Bill had a profound belief in evil because of the things he reported on. He tried so desperately to get away from them but found he couldn't. Was it possible that someone's torment and evil could actually seep into a place? For Bill, there was no doubt that not only was it possible, but there was proof in two different places: the former home of James and Susan Perry and the Devil Tree.

As strange as it sounded, he didn't mind having the company and wished she would speak again. Knowing he wasn't alone, by something non-malevolent communicating with him, with all this madness going on, provided him with a sense of comfort that was hard to explain.

According to Jim, his deceased wife had turned into a nasty woman the older she got and had become increasingly difficult to tolerate the further they grew apart.

Bill didn't experience her bad side he supposed because he wasn't married to her and didn't cause her unrest. He left her alone for the most part and respected her space on the other side of the house.

The police scanner came to life again, pulling Bill from his reverie. What he heard next pinned him to his seat and everything tingled.

"Your officer is down," a disgusting voice said. "He's given his life for the tree. There will be more. Stop me if you can."

The voice sounded like it was the embodiment of evil. Now he knew for sure it wasn't some curious kid roaming the forest. Something really bad had been unfolding at that tree.

Go now.

Contemplation no longer existed. Bill sprang into action and jumped to his feet. He grabbed his flashlight and exited the house.

As Bill took off into a full sprint, he knew his involvement was becoming more than a journalistic interest. It was about instructions from a dead woman in this house and a tree and the bad things that were happening there. The allure and the inability to shut off the scanner and stop writing blog posts about the dealings that were going on just beyond the C-24 canal sign proved that he was indeed in full service of the tree.

The bad omen that he mentioned was coming . . . maybe he felt it because it was coming for him, too.

Chapter 14

AFTERMATH

Bill hurried past the small C-24 canal fence and wasted no time reaching the path that would take him to the Devil Tree. His flashlight lit the way and his lungs burned from the full on sprint he had been running at since he left Susan and the house. Somehow, the strain of the physical exertion didn't slow him down because he needed to get to the tree and see for himself.

"Where the hell are the rest of the cops?" he said, panting as he slowed down. The time between when he heard the call from the officer and the sound of the demonic voice seemed like a long span of time. Bill looked at his watch; in reality it had only been a few minutes.

Bill shined the flashlight beam, scanning across the brush on either side of him, and when he came upon the tree he settled it on the naked body of a person hanging from one of the crooked tree limbs.

He gasped and staggered backward until he bumped into another tree, which kept him in place. His heart pounded from the run and skipped a beat from the shock and surprise of what he saw. The hand that held the flashlight shook terribly. When he lifted it and tried to steady it, he swept it over the dead man. Bill's eyes bulged and he covered his mouth to stifle a scream.

Rummaging through his pocket, he managed to locate his cell phone and access the camera. He turned on the flash and snapped a few pictures to see things better. The eerie scene lit up with the phone's bright spark, and more details came into focus and seared into his mind. Blood and guts were everywhere.

The sound of running feet that came from behind him wasn't enough to draw his attention away from what he saw. He had mind enough to put his phone away but didn't have the power to look away from the grizzly scene he stood approximately twenty feet away from.

"It's bad," he said, unsure of whom he was talking to. He didn't even know if the killer was behind him or if it was someone who had come to help the man he saw dangling from the tree.

No sooner did the words leave his mouth when Officer Abernathy ran past him.

"Damn it, no!" Officer Abernathy howled and reached for Lenza's body. "It's Lenza! They got Lenza!"

The panic and anger in Abernathy's voice was easy to hear.

"Look at what these bastards did to him!"

Bill watched on, unable to escape the horror. Abernathy struggled to lift the body, but the dead weight and pool of blood and guts on the ground made him slip.

"Don't just stand there! We need to cut him down." Abernathy looked into Bill's beam of light. "I'm talking to you! Get over here and help me get him down!"

Abernathy was covered in gore, and Bill couldn't go near that. He thought he knew what true evil was, but this . . . this was evil without a veil, and it was enough to change someone in an instant. That change was coming over Bill in giant waves of profound fear of what death must be like when it comes like this: paralyzing fear, agony, and the knowledge that it is inescapable. To imagine the loneliness as the darkness started to close in . . . the thoughts of things left undone and unsaid, never to be addressed because the last chance at life has been taken away.

Officer Breck wasn't far behind Abernathy and also rushed past Bill and sprang into action. He used his knife to cut through the thick rope that was used to string up the dead officer. Breck held onto the rope and eased the body down. Abernathy grabbed onto Lenza by the waist and guided him to the ground.

Bill kept his flashlight concentrated on the body, his mind in a state of shock. The officers . . . how could they look at scenes like this day after day and continue to function? How was it possible they could ever smile again knowing what evil was around them and their families?

"Let's get him out from underneath this tree," Abernathy said to Breck. Breck grabbed the fallen officer by the ankles and Abernathy took him under the arms. They moved him to flat ground that was away from the tree and the intrusive rooting system that bulged out of the earth.

"Give me your flashlight," Abernathy said to Bill, the officer's clothes and face now painted with his comrade's blood.

Bill didn't process a single word that was being said. All he could do was stand there, stuck inside his own head, knowing true fear as he looked into the maw of evil and tragedy.

He had seen the cavern in the man's belly and the guts that were strewn about the leaf-littered ground. The guts that hung from the branches were impossible to unsee and impossible to take in.

"Give me your damn light," Abernathy growled and tore Bill out of his trance. Bill tossed his light and Abernathy caught it.

The light went over every detail of the filleting. It illuminated the ground where the guts were spread around and then the tree where the tendrils were hung.

Abernathy dropped the flashlight and stormed over to Bill.

"Why are you always here right when shit like this happens?"

Bill searched for words, but the anger that distorted Abernathy's face and then was directed toward him was slow to register. He spread his hands to show his uncertainty. Finding the words that would explain how he got there so fast, how he ended up where they were, was impossible.

Abernathy was a big man and he towered over Bill. "I asked you a fucking question!" He lunged forward and grabbed Bill by the shoulders, shook him fiercely, and then flung him down to the ground. Bill landed awkwardly and hard in the thick brush. The bushes tore at his skin and seemed to want to hold him in place. It was better he didn't stand up anyway.

"Abernathy, stop!" Breck called out and ran over to him. "We've got enough shit to worry about besides a two-bit reporter sitting on top of his scanner." He took Abernathy by the arm and led him away.

The body, the guts, the tree, death, and the thrashing he just took were all things Bill looked at over and over again in his mind's eye.

"You're a piece of shit, Bill, do you hear me?"

"You can't think I had anything to do with this!" Bill said and tried to stand, but the branches tugged at his clothing and reminded him to stay down.

"Maybe not, but I think you know exactly what is going on here," Abernathy shouted and tried to wrestle away from Breck's grasp. Breck stood his ground, but Abernathy shouted, "You're lucky he's here or I'd hang you from that damn tree myself!"

The threat didn't worry Bill. Abernathy was in shock and was directing his anger toward him because he was the only one there he could do that to.

"It's just like your partner said. I heard it over the police scanner I have in my house. You know I live around the corner."

Abernathy sneered. "You live in that fucking house! Why in the hell would you buy that? What sort of sick individual buys a house where a man killed his wife?"

"I don't know."

"You don't know, but you specifically sought that place out. Don't you remember I was attacked there by the man who lived there?"

"I remember . . ." The blood stain came to mind.

"That man was driven crazy by whatever he saw by this tree, and he killed his wife with his own bare hands while I lay there unconscious just a few feet away from him."

"I know."

"I carry that shit around with me!"

Bill stood shakily. The slamming he had taken made him unsteady.

"This is for real, Bill. Bad things happen here, and I dream about what happened every time I close my eyes. The feeling that I am to blame for some of this inserts itself into my every day. Knowing I couldn't do anything to save that woman's life because I was too blind to see what was right in front of me. It happened twice! But this time I'm watching with eyes wide open, and every time I look, I see you in front of me."

Bill remained silent, mulling the words, understanding where Abernathy was coming from.

"Don't you hear what I'm saying to you?" Abernathy said. "A man snapped and killed his wife, and you go and buy his house! Why would you do that?"

Bill looked at the tree and the chaos all around him. Abernathy was in a blind rage, probably driven that way by his friend being strung up and by being around the tree again.

"It's the tree," Bill said. "It has something to do with the tree." He looked inward while he hung onto Abernathy's words, and there he found the evil he was so afraid of. It was in his actions.

"If you know what this thing is, then why are you there in that house of all places?"

"I don't know. I felt like I needed to be there."

"What for, Bill? Tell me what for!"

"I . . . I don't know."

"Why are you always here when something goes to shit?"

"I'm trying to give you an answer." Bill's voice fell flat. "I think it's because of that tree. I think your anger and my curiosity, the actions of the killers—they're all a direct result of that tree and what Schaeffer did here. I can't explain it."

"I want you to stay right here," Abernathy said. "And don't you dare lay eyes on that officer over there. He's one of ours, and how he lays there right now is a disgrace to his good name and memory. God help you if you report what you've seen here. This badge won't mean a damn thing to me."

"I understand," Bill said and looked at the ground by his feet.

"Do you really think you understand?" Abernathy said and waved a dismissive hand at Bill. "Ah, to hell with you and to whoever is doing this."

"I'm sorry this happened."

Abernathy looked all around and then bared his teeth as he spoke to Bill. "I have questions for you, and that means you are going to have to wait to make your next blog post. You can continue to stir things up and pull crazy people out of the woodwork, but not until I get to ask you some more questions."

"I'll answer anything you need."

"I know you will because you are a suspect in a very serious crime investigation."

"I don't need a lawyer, and I won't remain silent because I have nothing to hide."

"I wasn't going to offer you one, and if I feel you're holding out on me . . ."

Abernathy had a crazed look about him, and Bill couldn't blame him. Abernathy had been Schaeffer's partner and didn't know he was killing people at this tree. Now others were killing more of his friends in Schaeffer's name. It was like they were mocking him, and it played on his emotions. This was turning him into something he wasn't.

"I'll cooperate in any way I can," Bill said and saw that his arms trickled blood and his back hurt from the odd way he landed. The stiff poking of the unforgiving branches probably tore up his back. "I am as perplexed and concerned about this as you are. I'm sorry."

"You're sorry?" Abernathy seethed. "Is that so, Bill? So you knew that man lying on the ground over there? You've seen one of your friends hollowed out by a bunch of savages and hanged from a tree?"

"No, that's not what I meant."

"I suppose you got to stand up for him as his best man? You know his wife and kid?"

"No."

"Maybe you should go to his house and tell his wife what happened to him. How about you do that and see how well you sleep tonight?"

Breck tugged on Abernathy's shoulder, but Abernathy just shrugged him off. "I want him to answer my question."

Bill remained silent. He was concerned that his answer might provoke Abernathy even more.

"Are you going to be the one to go and do that and catch his wife when the shock of that message hits her so hard she won't be able to stand, and she wails out in anguish as she tries to understand what her husband went through and that he's never going to come back?"

"No, of course not," Bill whispered.

"No, of course not," Abernathy mocked. "You get to hide behind a computer screen where you are all safe and sound, stirring up the shit instead of having to be on the front lines risking your life and dealing with this shit. I can't stand people like you."

"I'm sorry . . . I don't know what to say."

"Neither do I," Abernathy said. "But stop telling me you're sorry. It's like I said. I'm looking at the things right in front of me, and I think you might know something that you're not telling me."

Bill didn't answer that. Abernathy's frustration rose when he spoke. Seeing a fallen comrade only intensified his anger and exposed his hopelessness in all the chaos that had begun to surround this tree again.

Bill understood it wasn't Abernathy. He trusted him and knew he was a good cop. He didn't harbor any hard feelings toward the officer about having been shoved or even being accused of knowing something about what happened here. The only things he wanted were the same answers the police were after. And once Abernathy allowed him to leave, he would continue on his quest to try to solve the riddle of who the killer was and help bring them to justice. If he didn't do that, he wouldn't be able to sleep ever again.

Chapter 15

FOLLOWING LEADS

There were no further questions from Abernathy. He moved far away from Bill and broke down in tears over his fallen friend over by the police car. Officer Breck told Bill to leave and that he was sorry for his partner's outburst—that he had been angry at everything around him and not Bill specifically.

Bill understood that the work of a police officer was tough, and now that he saw what they went through up close, he had an idea of how taxing it really was both physically and mentally. It was something he couldn't imagine doing himself.

He returned home and rested his elbows on his knees. Night had turned to day as he tried to focus his mind on his next task.

Taking the phone from his pocket, he swiped through the pictures he'd snapped of the naked officer dangling from the tree. Nausea wrapped his stomach in a tight knot, and he clamped his eyes shut and tried to control his breathing. Panic was creeping into the mix.

He sent the pictures to his email account, retrieved them, and printed them out to have a better look. The details were sickening, but he felt it necessary that he look everything over to make sure he wasn't missing any important details that might give him a lead.

The officer's blue face, the head tilted to the side, and the big dark hole in his abdomen were impossible to look at. Bill lowered the picture, unsure if he could study it any longer. What could drive a person to do something so sadistic? The agony the officer endured must have been unspeakable. To imagine that evil descending with a big sharp knife and being unable to do anything to escape it made him shiver. Bill could only hope the officer had passed out from shock.

He couldn't get himself to look at the photographs anymore so he dropped the pictures on his desk face down. He grabbed his digital recorder, rewound it, and listened to Abernathy and Captain Moore revealing the names of the women who found the body buried underneath the ancient oak a few days ago. Was that yesterday? The days were a blur.

Bill remembered seeing their silhouettes in the back of Abernathy's squad car. The torment trapped in there must have been terrible.

He grabbed a random piece of paper and scribbled their names on it. Shutting off the recorder, he went to the Google search engine on his computer and typed in the first name mentioned: Bridget Linne.

Wikipedia popped up with the search result, but with the killer, Schaeffer, listed as the main article. He clicked on the link and began to read. Underneath the 'capture' header, it revealed that Bridget Linne was one of the two girls Schaeffer had tried to abduct and bring to the Devil Tree, only for them to escape and seek the help of the police. The article went on to say that Bridget was prolific in mixed martial arts and used that to her advantage to allow her and her friend, Elizabeth Brown, to escape unscathed. Elizabeth Brown was the other name captured on the recorder.

They ultimately identified Schaeffer at the police precinct when they saw his deputy picture hanging on the wall. Bill searched for Bridget's address, and it came up instantly. Three miles of separation between his residence and her last known address would be easy to cover. Wasting no time, he grabbed his recorder, notepad with a pen, and his cell phone. He got up and walked out the door, heading for Bridget's home, hoping to get some answers as to what she saw when she discovered the body—and what the police told her, if anything.

Bill walked up to the stucco home located on a quiet street where newly constructed homes were popping up one after the other.

Drawing a deep breath, he took in some courage and knocked on the door. A few moments later, the door swung open, and a young man aged around twenty-five to thirty answered the door. He wore a long-sleeved shirt, and a tattoo snaked out of his shirt and crawled up the side of his neck. It ended just before his ear.

"Yeah?" the guy said, manners clearly not his strong suit.

"How are you doing?" Bill said, hoping to put the man at ease. "My name is Bill Faulkner. May I ask you your name, sir?"

"Dalton," he said, and he folded his arms across his chest. "Dalton Vyle."

"Dalton, I'm a local reporter, and this is the last known address for a Ms. Bridget Linne. I was hoping that if she's home I could have an opportunity to have a few words with her."

"What do you want to speak to her about?" Dalton said, his face crinkling into suspicion.

"I want to know what happened yesterday at the Devil Tree. I'm hoping she would be willing to share her knowledge with me."

Dalton shook his head and grabbed the door, ready to close it. "She's all shook up, and she doesn't want to talk to anyone. I'd like you to leave."

"No, wait," Bridget said from somewhere deep within the house. She walked to the door. "Did you say your name was Bill Faulkner?"

"Yes."

"I've been reading your coverage on the Devil Tree and I think it's very good. I mean, I think you're onto something and I don't mind talking to you."

"Excellent. Thank you," Bill said. "Would you like to come out here and talk or should I come inside?"

"I'd like to come out," Bridget said. "Maybe we can take a walk around the block. It'll allow me to get some much needed fresh air. I've been in the house since we discovered the body, and I think getting out might do me some good."

Dalton stepped back from the door so she could pass.

Bridget exited the house, and she began to walk. Bill hurried to catch her and stay by her side. He waited until they walked about a half a block away before he felt comfortable enough to ask her his questions.

"May I ask what you were doing at the tree?"

Bridget breathed deeply. "I was there with my friend, Elizabeth."

"Elizabeth Brown?"

"Yes, along with me, she was the other person originally kidnapped by Schaeffer and brought to the park."

"But because of your background in mixed martial arts you were able to escape?"

"I was. Thank God for the time I spent training. I didn't want to do it, but my parents kind of made me. In a way, I suppose they saved my life." She walked in silence. "I can't tell you how many times I wanted to quit, but my parents encouraged me to stay with it . . . my father in particular. I look at it as a kid being a kid. I really resented him and the way he pushed me at the time. But now I wish he was around to thank because it saved my life."

"Do you mind if I record our conversation? I use it to help me remember what we spoke about and what to put into my next blog entry."

"Go right ahead," Bridget said. "I don't mind at all. Maybe sharing my story might help someone else out there."

"I appreciate that. Do you mind telling me what made you go back to the Devil Tree? I mean, was it calling to you? Maybe it had you curious or something?"

"No, it was nothing like that," Bridget said. "Elizabeth has been having nightmares about our abduction or whatever you want to call it. I think I was able to come to terms with what had happened a lot quicker than her. I understand there are bad people in the world. The one we ran into was something worse than bad. I think he was the definition of evil. I remember the look in his eyes. I swear he had no soul."

"Did she tell you what sort of nightmares she was having?"

"Only one," Bridget said and picked up a stick. It was the perfect size to use as a walking stick. "She doesn't get too much into detail, but from what I was able to get out of her: Schaeffer gets her to the tree and has this ivory-handled knife or something, and he's tormenting her with it. He would press the blade into her skin and get so close that she could smell his breath within the dream. She said she could feel something evil lurking in the tree and looking down on her, but she can never see what it is."

Bill shook his head. "That sounds frightening."

"The poor girl shakes when she talks about it. That's why I try to change the subject if she tries to get too far into it. I told her she should see a doctor, but she refuses. I was there, so I know how frightening it was and can understand her fear."

"I don't suppose she could ask for a better friend," Bill said. He wanted to get into the meat and potatoes of his questioning. "So why did you two go to the tree, exactly?"

"We went there to try to find some closure. We bought some flowers we were going to set at the base of the tree. Then we planned to offer some prayers to the people who perished there in hopes that they were able to move on. We knew they were probably having difficulty doing that seeing as we are alive and are having a hard time moving on from it. To perish at the end of his blade while being tormented has got to be something else entirely."

"So you believe in ghosts?"

"I guess it would be too simple to just say yes." Bridget sighed. "I believed there was evil out in the world, but I never understood how evil someone could actually be until that night I looked into Schaeffer's eyes. Like I said, there was something wicked about him. I'm not sure if there was just something wrong with him or if he opened the door to something iniquitous because he practiced Satanism and it attached itself to him. I believe the trauma of what he did left a stain behind, and that has left people's souls to wander."

"I believe that to be true, too," Bill said as he thought about Susan roaming the house that was once hers.

They had gone full circle and were standing in front of Bridget's house. She discarded the stick and faced Bill. "Did I answer all of your questions, Mr. Faulkner?"

"Yes you did, but as I stand here and look into your eyes, I see fear . . . and I want to know if what I see is rooted inside of you now?"

Bridget looked away for a moment. "Yes, I am fearful of that tree and the things that go on there. I don't like that I have somehow become a part of this, and I hope someday soon it is over for me. I just want to live in peace. Find the good in people and maybe have a family of my own one day. I just want to be normal."

"I understand that and hope you get what you're seeking." He looked down the street and then back at Bridget. "Do you think Elizabeth would be open to talking to me?"

"I think so, but I can't say so for sure."

"No, of course not. I know you can't speak for her."

The front door opened and Dalton Vyle stepped outside. "You've been with him long enough, Bridget. Why don't you come inside?"

"We were just finishing up now."

"I'm not thrilled with you talking to any damn reporter— especially him."

"Please excuse him," Bridget whispered to Bill. "He just stopped by to see how I was doing, and I think his intentions are good. He's a bit overprotective of me and Elizabeth is all."

"I don't want these guys putting things out there that should be left alone," Dalton said. "They wouldn't know discretion if it slapped them upside the head."

"I don't suppose my voice was low enough," she said to Bill. She moved her lips close to his ear, and when she spoke it gave Bill the chills. "Thank you for stopping by. Even though Dalton doesn't want us talking, I'm glad we did. It felt good to have someone's ear that actually listens."

"Who is he?"

"He's a friend from school I had lost touch with. Facebook put us back in touch after all these years. He's been coming around and checking on me and Elizabeth since that whole thing went down with Schaeffer."

Bill looked at Dalton, and something about him repulsed Bill. It wasn't entirely dissimilar to the feeling he got when he was around the tree.

Dalton stared with a hardened look for a few uncomfortable moments and then turned away and walked inside the house. Bill tried not to show that it bothered him and turned his attention back to Bridget.

"I thank you for talking with me. I know it must be difficult. You're a very brave woman."

He shook her hand and walked away, and strangely, nothing about the conversation stuck in his mind. But that Dalton guy . . . the way he looked and handled himself just rubbed Bill the wrong way. He would have to figure out who he was.

Chapter 16

SCOURING THE AREA

"You don't really think that blogger, Bill, actually had anything to do with this, do you?" Breck said.

They were still at the tree, and the crime scene team was placing Officer Lenza's desecrated body into a black bag. Some poor son of a bitch was following around a photographer and collecting the body parts that were scattered all around the tree. He was placing them in smaller bags and handing them off to a third person, who wrote on the bags.

"No," Abernathy said. "That was anger at what I saw, nothing more. I owe him an apology, and when I see him, that's exactly what I'm going to do."

"When the time is right," Breck said. "He knew. I could see it in his face, and he told me so. That's the first time I ever saw you lose your cool."

"And the last. If I let them get to me like that I'm not thinking rationally, and that could impede on my ability to find what isn't obvious and help solve these crimes."

Breck and Abernathy scoured the area around the tree and even started to penetrate the nearby thicket to make sure no clues were left behind.

"I don't know," Abernathy said. "I suppose when I saw Schaeffer jump out of the tree and break his neck, and then I had the priest perform an exorcism and I patched the tree to cover the occult writings, I felt that was it. There was closure wrapped up in a small package that I could try to put away. But I knew I would never forget. I'm distracted and fearful that this won't go away. I'm being driven by anger and fear instead of unrelenting persistence that'll put away whoever did this to Lenza and the girl who was dismembered and buried at the tree. The girls who got away from Schaeffer didn't deserve to be the ones to find that. They've been affected as much as me, if not more."

"I think you should cut yourself some slack. There's someone running around . . . the way things are, I don't know . . . I'm guessing there are a lot of people that are part of this. Damn Schaeffer freaks using the tree as an excuse to act like animals."

"Bill was right. It has as much to do with the tree as it does Schaeffer. Look at the way they chiseled out that cement patch to expose his writings. The tree is a catalyst planted deep in the soil, and we gave up and left it here. That was a mistake. We should have ripped it down by any means necessary."

"But the equipment all malfunctioned."

"We could have brought in a damn Bobcat or something. We could have stuck the forks underneath the rooting system and pulled it out of the ground that way." Abernathy grabbed his temples and rubbed. "We had to know it was going to attract people like this. I wasn't thinking ahead, and now Lenza paid for it."

"How could we know that?" Breck said. "How could you hope to know that?"

Breck used his baton to plow through the thicket. Sticks snapped as he cleared a path.

Abernathy watched Breck. "Because we are the police, and we are supposed to account for things like that. Leaving Lenza out here on night shift all alone was a mistake."

"I can't argue with that." Breck canvassed the area but didn't come up with anything. "So what's next?"

"I don't know." Abernathy went in the opposite direction as Breck and used the same tactic to get through the heavy overgrowth. He stopped. "Breck, you may want to come over here, quick."

Breck hurried out of the thicket he managed to weave himself into and crashed through the growth where Abernathy stood.

Two bloody mattresses were in a small clearing surrounded by bushes and bent, runty trees. They were woven together to form a shelter.

"What the hell is this?" Breck said.

"Go get someone from the forensics team and show them this," Abernathy said and pushed himself forward. The vegetation became even thicker, and the ability to move forward in a straight line was not only difficult but at times impossible.

Somehow he managed to break free of the branch-covered passageway and come upon a deteriorated frame ripped down to ground level. Cinderblock, moss, and overgrown vegetation concealed what he thought had been a tiny house.

"What in the hell is this doing out here?"

Abernathy walked the perimeter of the cinderblock frame. Broken beer bottles and graffiti defiled the ruins. A wood-rotted and knotted chicken wire fence was trampled. The ground, covered with packed dirt, leaves, and flat rocks that may have served as flooring at one time, kept his attention. It seemed out of place, but so did the ruins.

"Hey, Breck?"

"Yeah?"

He was behind him, hanging back with the forensics person at the mattresses. Abernathy stared at the flat rocks with an aching curiosity he soon dismissed. It was just a floor of flat rock.

"Never mind," he said.

"What is it?"

"Nothing."

Abernathy looked all around and saw multiple frames of ruined houses. It was strange how he never noticed them before. It was obvious they had been there a long time.

He turned away to return to Breck and the person from forensics without another thought to the presence of the ruins. He wanted to see what they had discovered in the makeshift shelter.

Chapter 17

ELIZABETH

Bill approached Elizabeth's front door and knocked. The door swung open as if she was expecting him. His first thought was that Bridget had tipped her off to his coming. He supposed it was better this way.

The last thing Elizabeth needed was to be surprised by his arrival and him sniffing around with questions she might not want to answer. According to Bridget, Elizabeth was having a harder time coping with what happened to them at the hands of Schaeffer.

He looked at her: a tall, slender young woman with deep blue eyes and cherry red hair; she smiled at him through the screen door.

"You must be Bill," she said.

"I am," he said, glad that he didn't have to try to wiggle his way in to gain her trust. It seemed his hunch was right and Bridget had already taken care of the difficult part for him.

She opened the door and held it for him. "Please, come in so we can sit."

Bill entered the small apartment that was neat but unassuming in every way. A few pictures of tranquil settings decorated the wall; a loveseat, flat screen television mounted on the wall, and four chairs surrounded a rectangular table. The windows didn't have drapes, and the walls were stark white.

"Bridget called me and told me to expect you," she said. "I know this may sound a bit strange, but I'm glad you came here and are giving me the opportunity to talk about what happened. Maybe it will help me come to terms with what I experienced . . . and maybe then I can move on. Bridget is a few steps ahead of me, and I'd like to catch up to her. Maybe I can help someone else if they find themselves in the same situation as Bridget and me."

Her eyes looked sad, and there was a palpable nervousness that followed her; Bill could hear it in her unconvincing words and see it in her eyes. She tried to appear brave, but she wasn't.

"Thank you for talking to me," Bill said, mentally noting that her worry was deeper than Bridget's—and she had said exactly what Bridget said about wanting to help other people. That was probably the argument Bridget used to get her to talk to him.

"After my run-in with the killer deputy, I spent an awful lot of time sitting in this apartment, afraid to go outside and scared to fall asleep because I kept having the same nightmare over and over again."

"Do you mind talking about this nightmare? Maybe you can share some of the details with me?"

Elizabeth clasped her hands and then rubbed her palms together. She clenched her jaw and took a deep breath.

"After the fact, I heard what he did to that guy and girl at the tree before he kidnapped us. Although I don't know all the details of what he did, I often dream that he has us at the tree and has this real evil look on his face. I've never told Bridget that she's there with me. I don't want to upset her. Anyway, Schaeffer is dressed as a woman and is holding this knife. I can feel all sorts of things that I can't explain that are coming from Schaeffer and the tree. More so the tree, I think. Whatever it is and wherever it is coming from, it is evil. It always ends with the tree coming alive. The branches become hands, and a face forms on the tree trunk. Bridget and I run away, but it always catches her. It trips me, and I crawl to try and get away, but it grabs my ankles, and that's when I wake up." She laughed. "It sounds so stupid, I know."

"No, it doesn't," Bill said. "It is totally understandable considering what you went through and what you know about the tree. You and Bridget were very lucky. It is believed that Schaeffer may have killed in excess of thirty-six people."

"Wow," Elizabeth said and reared her head, her eyes getting wide as she took in what he said. "That's a lot of people. A lot of torment and pain he inflicted."

"Yes it is. He got away with it for a long time. I guess you can say he met his match when he picked you and Bridget up."

"I suppose," she said. "More so Bridget because she's the one that beat him up." Elizabeth chuckled.

"I'm wondering why you and Bridget went to the tree the other day. I mean, with your nightmares and fear of the tree, I would think you would want to stay as far away from there as you could."

"I do, but I wanted to face my fears in hopes of being able to put it behind me. I wanted to know for sure the tree wasn't going to grow arms and grab me by my ankles." Her eyes welled with tears. "We both wanted to put the tree behind us but it seems the devil's curse on that tree wouldn't have it."

"It wasn't the tree that did that to those people."

"Maybe not," she said. "But people who talk about the tree say it has a certain draw to it. You even say that in your blog posts. It influences people to do things like that old man Perry guy. It's like they can't stay away from it or something. If they do, they go bonkers. Now we have people killing people at the tree in that guy's name. Where is the end to this?"

"The police will catch them."

"I hope so," Elizabeth said. "I'd like this mindless dedication to evil to go away. It's a tree. Just a tree, right?"

"Yes, it's just a tree," Bill lied. "What can you tell me about this Dalton Vyle guy who hangs around Bridget?"

"Her boyfriend?"

"Is he her boyfriend?"

"Yeah. I mean I think so. They spend an awful lot of time together. He started coming around after the Schaeffer incident. He friended us on Facebook and started coming around. I think it's sweet that he tries to protect us . . . even if he weirds me out a little.

"Even though she has that innocent look about her, she's always had this thing for bad boys," Elizabeth said and shook her head. "I try to tell her over and over again that even though his intentions seem nice now, he's the kind of guy who's probably no good for her. But, she wants what she wants. He seems like he's trying to help. Anytime I tell her that he gives me the creeps, she gets mad, and that seems to be interfering in our friendship."

"Well I can tell you that I didn't get a good feeling from him either," Bill said. "I don't mean to sound judgmental, and I can't explain it. He just felt off to me."

"I think you got that exactly right. I don't get a good feeling from him either."

Bill put away his notepad and shut off his voice recorder. "I want to thank you for talking to me, and I hope you find closure to all of this."

"That'll come once the police solve the murder," Elizabeth said. She got up and walked Bill to the door. "Please don't tell her that I told you that Dalton was her boyfriend. I don't want her to get angry and never talk to me again—she's the only friend I have."

"I promise," Bill said. "Again, thank you for talking with me."

"No problem," she said and wiped her wet eyes and gently closed the door as Bill exited the apartment.

Chapter 18

BREAKING THE LAW

"You guys know the drill by now," Breck said. "We can't comment on an ongoing investigation."

The flock of reporters was like a gang of hungry hounds pulling against their master's leash, trying to stay on the trail.

"Is it true items were found by the tree and they might have been used during the execution of Officer Lenza?" a reporter said.

"No comment. We can't talk about it. Comprende?"

Bill approached the familiar yellow tape that went across the C-24 canal sign. Abernathy locked eyes with him and ordered the reporters back who were attempting to move the boundary forward.

"You see this yellow tape?" Abernathy said with a firm tone. "You're not to push against it. It is here for a reason, and that is to keep you guys back and out of the way so we can do our jobs."

"One of your own died," a reporter somewhere in the middle of the mix said. "How is that you doing your jobs?"

Abernathy's face burned red from anger, and Breck stepped in and made the reporters back up about a foot.

Abernathy stood there with his jaw tight and a subtle shake to his body. "Whoever said that should learn discretion and respect. You're a fucking shark."

Abernathy walked over to Bill and lifted the yellow tape.

"Come with me and let's talk."

The gaggle of reporters voiced their protest, but Officer Breck took control over them, giving Abernathy the opportunity to make things right with the blogger.

"I owe you an apology," Abernathy said to Bill. He had him in the same spot where Bill had dropped his voice recorder.

"No you don't," Bill said.

"I do. I put my hands on you in anger, and I should never have done that."

"It's OK," Bill said. "Believe me, I understand. One of your officers was killed and you were angry and frustrated. I was there when I shouldn't have been."

"So we're good?"

"We are good," Bill said. "But that isn't the reason I came here today."

Abernathy looked at the gathering of reporters and made sure the distance from them to him and Bill was sufficient enough to keep them from picking up on what they were talking about. He didn't see any parabolic dishes so he felt they were at a safe distance.

"I did something you're not going to be very happy about, but I believe the end result was worth the risk on my end," Bill said.

"What is it?" Abernathy said and shifted his weight from one foot to the other.

"The girls who found the body by the tree and were sitting in your squad car that night . . . I asked you who they were and you wouldn't tell me. Do you remember that?"

"Of course I do."

"I understand why you have to do that, and please try to understand that I report the news, and sometimes I do things . . . make decisions to get the story no matter what. I do things that maybe I shouldn't do."

"What did you do, Bill?"

"Sometimes I walk a thin line between what is right and wrong—ethical and unethical—to get answers."

"I get it," Abernathy said. He folded his arms across his chest. "Let's get to why you are here."

"I don't know if you remember or not, but when the first bodies were discovered by Jim Perry, I had some information no one else had. I gained that information by hiding in bushes nearby well before any of the other reporters had gathered."

Abernathy looked at his feet, to the crowd of reporters, then back at Bill. He was holding his tongue.

"You took me to this very spot to talk to me, to shut me up and promise me some information at a later date. I agreed to that. But this time I couldn't wait. I don't know why; I just couldn't. When you wouldn't give me the girls' names, I tossed a voice-activated recorder right here and captured the conversation you had with the captain. I got the names of the girls who discovered the bodies."

"You planted a recorder?" Abernathy shook his head. "You're confessing to a crime, Bill."

"I know I am. But what you need to know is I found out where both girls live and I went to interview them."

Abernathy placed his hands on his hips, sighed, pinched the bridge of his nose, and chuckled.

"Please, listen to what I have to say."

Abernathy nodded. "OK, Bill, I'm listening."

"What the girls told me is everything you already know. They came here for closure and found the newly dug grave. Fast forward. When I went to Bridget's house, there was this guy there. His name is Dalton Vyle. He had tattoos running up the side of his neck and he just seemed off to me. He wore long sleeves—"

"So?"

"It was weird. I felt like he was hiding something. Bridget told me he was just a friend from high school who started coming around after they had a run-in with Schaeffer. I went to interview Elizabeth, and she said this guy was Bridget's boyfriend. I mean why would she hide that?"

Abernathy pulled at his chin, looked over his shoulder, and then returned his attention to Bill. "I'm still listening. You have me now, Bill. Give me something good."

"I can't explain it. I just had a bad feeling about him."

"OK. Where was the last place you saw this Dalton Vyle?"

"I saw him at Bridget's house. This guy guarded her and the doorway of the house like a sentinel. He wouldn't let me talk to her. It was like he was trying to stonewall me. She heard me though and came outside to talk."

"How long ago did this take place?"

"About two hours. No more than that."

Abernathy thought for a moment, and Bill tapped his foot, waiting.

"I think you should go question him or something," Bill said. "Maybe you can stop by and say you're checking on Bridget to see how she's doing or something."

Abernathy nodded.

"I'm telling you, there's something off about that guy."

"Go home, Bill. Don't be a part of this flock behind the yellow tape. Thank you for the information. I'll let you know what comes of it."

Abernathy went over to Breck and pulled him aside. "I'm going to follow up on a lead Bill just gave me. I'll radio it in on my way. I don't have time to explain."

He ducked underneath the yellow tape and made his own path through the crowd of reporters. He got into his patrol car and Bill watched him belt himself in and pull away, his tires spitting dirt as he did so.

Chapter 09

DALTON VYLE

Abernathy pulled in front of Bridget's house and radioed dispatch.

"Ten-ninety-seven," he said.

"Ten-four," dispatch responded.

He exited the vehicle, walked across the lawn, and looked down both sides of the house. He went to the front door and knocked, resting his hand on the butt of his 9mm.

The events that transpired when Jim attacked him were always fresh on his mind, and whenever he found himself walking into a situation he was unclear about, he took a step back and evaluated the circumstances a little more closely than he used to. He didn't want to make any fatal errors.

The door opened, and a young man fitting the description Bill gave him stared back at him.

"Yeah?" Dalton said.

"I had a disturbance call from this residence," Abernathy said. "Is anyone else inside the house?"

The leather on the officer's utility belt squeaked with each movement. His bulletproof vest made his torso thick, and the bright day cast his massive shadow over Dalton.

"Yeah, but she's in the bathroom. What's this all about?"

"The girl in the bathroom, can you tell me what her name is?"

"Bridget."

"How do you know her?"

"I know her from back in school. She's a friend of mine I've recently reconnected with."

"I need you to step outside."

"Step outside? For what reason?"

"Like I said, I had a disturbance call come in, and I'd like to make sure everyone is OK. Now step out of the house and keep your hands where I can see them."

"A disturbance call from this house?" Dalton laughed. "Bridget is fine, and we haven't made so much as a peep. What is this, bad cop shows up to bust my balls?"

"Step outside, sir, or I'm going to come in and get you out," Abernathy said. Being much bigger than Dalton, Abernathy was confident that if he needed to take him down it would be quick. "I'm not going to ask you again."

A negative vibe exactly as Bill described oozed off of Dalton and reached Abernathy on the other side of the doorway. It made him uneasy, and he grasped the handle of his 9mm dependently. Something was afoul here, and he needed to maintain control over the situation at all times and figure out what it was.

Dalton stepped outside and Abernathy unclipped the strap that went over his pistol. His hand wrapped the gun again and his finger was placed in a position that would allow him to draw his weapon and pump out several rounds quickly if need be.

"Why are you harassing me?"

"Do you have any ID?"

"What do I need ID for? I'm in my friend's house minding my own business. You come over here making up some bullshit story about a disturbance call."

Abernathy tried to look past Dalton to see if he could spot anyone else inside the house, but the bright sun kept the house dark.

"I'd like to see your ID. It's a simple request."

"I don't have it on me."

"Is it in the house?"

Dalton shook his head and smiled. He looked at his feet and to the left and right of Abernathy. Abernathy noticed he had sneakers on.

"Don't even think about running. You don't stand a chance, and it'd cause you a bunch of pain."

"I have no reason to run, and I don't appreciate you threatening me," Dalton said.

"Turn around and put your hands behind your back. Your behavior is making me feel uneasy, do you understand that?"

"No."

"Are you under the influence of any narcotics?"

"Not yet." Dalton laughed.

"I'm going to detain you until I figure out what is going on here and make sure everything checks out."

The hand that didn't hug the gun hovered over Dalton's shoulder just in case he decided to run. Dalton hesitated to obey the command but eventually turned around and put his hands behind his back. He rested his forehead on the front door's frame, and Abernathy kicked Dalton's feet apart.

"I'm obeying your commands so why don't you go a little easier? I know there was no call," Dalton said. "This is because of that reporter guy who came snooping around earlier, isn't it?"

"What reporter guy?" Abernathy said and grabbed Dalton's thumbs with one hand and patted him down with the other. He lifted Dalton's sleeves to get the cuffs on him, and Abernathy saw a pentagram on one forearm and on the other forearm he easily recognized the Goat of Mendes.

"I'm only detaining you at this time. I'm going to place you in the back of my patrol car for your safety and my own."

"Yeah, sure. For my safety and yours, I get it."

Abernathy walked him to the car, searched his person a second time, and placed him in the back seat. "Do you want to tell me what the tats are about?"

"Why, is there a law against my tattoos all of a sudden?"

"No, but I find it suspicious that you have a pentagram and the Goat of Mendes on your arms. There's been satanic activity in the area, and maybe it's a coincidence you have them. I'm curious to know what else is underneath that shirt."

"You know the names of symbols on my arms, I'm impressed."

"A specialty of mine," Abernathy said. The occult was something he studied extensively before he settled into the Port Saint Lucie Police Department. It was something he'd had great interest in once, but that soon waned when he decided to settle into a smaller city and have a family and a life outside of work. The Schaeffer case had been hindering that as of late.

"So, like, what are you gonna do? Strip search me or something because I have tats you don't like?"

"No, I'm not going to touch you because I'm not a bad cop. I believe in the law."

Abernathy slammed the back door and walked to Bridget's door.

"Bridget?" he said, walking in through the open front door.

Bridget emerged from the bathroom. "Officer Abernathy!"

"Are you OK?"

"Yes, why?"

"I know Bill was here earlier, and he told me about this guy, Dalton Vyle. Bill had a bad vibe from him and told me I should check things out. The guy out in my car fits the description Bill gave me. Can you confirm who he is?" Abernathy stepped to the side and nodded toward his car.

"His name is Dalton Vyle."

Abernathy wrote the name down. "Who is he to you?"

"He's just a friend from school. I hadn't seen him in years and just reconnected with him through Facebook. He started coming around soon after that. Why?"

"Did you know he has satanic tattoos on his arms?"

"What? No," Bridget said, and her concern spread across her face.

"What was he doing here?"

"He said he was just stopping by before he went to his friend's house. He said he was checking on me, and we had lunch together."

Abernathy nodded. "He's no good, Bridget, and you need to be careful who you're letting into your home."

"We were friends in high school. He seemed genuinely concerned about my well-being. I just trusted him because I knew him from years ago."

Abernathy stared at his patrol car, and Dalton was looking back at him, his tongue flickering like a snake's.

"I have a thirteen-P," Abernathy said into his radio. "I think he may be a sixty-four. Dalton Vyle, copy."

"Ten-four."

"When did he come over?" Abernathy said to Bridget.

"This morning . . . sometime after breakfast. I don't know. I kind of thought it weird that he stopped by without calling me or messaging me first, but I dismissed that because I just figured he was in the area. He's done it before."

"He's a ten-forty-nine," dispatch said. "He has a thirty-nine."

"Ten-four," Abernathy said into the radio. He looked at Bridget. "He has a warrant out for his arrest."

Bridget just stared, blinking as she processed this new information.

"It's for assault. That guy out there is a criminal. Like I said, be mindful of what you're doing, Bridget. There are dangerous people out there, and you're associated with the tree they're fixated on. I'm telling you, activity at the tree has picked up again, but I'm still not sure what's going on. I'll be in touch. Be safe, and call me if you need anything."

Abernathy walked to the car and cracked open the back door. "You have a warrant for your arrest."

"What for?"

"Assault. Don't play games, Dalton, you know."

"Yeah," Dalton said and laughed. "I suppose I do."

Abernathy read Dalton his Miranda rights.

"Yeah, yeah," Dalton said. "Maybe you should add murder to that charge while you're at it," he muttered.

Abernathy yanked the door open fully. "What did you just say?"

Dalton closed his eyes and rested his head back.

"I asked you what you just said."

"I have the right to remain silent, don't I?"

Abernathy didn't answer that. He wanted to yank him out of the car and beat the hell out of him. It took everything he had to close the door and walk around his patrol car and climb into the driver's seat.

"I didn't do anything to her because I figured that reporter guy sensed something was up. Her time was close, and now that I look back, I should have done what needed to be done, knowing my gig was up. I mean, I had plenty of time to do it."

"What were you going to do to her?"

Dalton lifted his head and smiled, meeting Abernathy's eyes in the rearview mirror.

"I was going to take her to the tree and kill her. I was going to make her suffer."

Abernathy gripped the steering wheel until his knuckles turned white. He drove toward the precinct with haste, contemplating pulling over and beating the shit out of the guy. He could always say he'd tried to resist arrest. But no matter how angry Lenza's death made him, how angry the tree seemed to make him, he was still a cop and needed to uphold the law.

"I don't believe you," Abernathy said, hiding his anger. "First, I think she'd kick your ass."

"Yeah, well, not if she's not looking."

"Second, you're giving me too much information willingly. You're not making me work for it."

"I'm proud of what I've done, and it's the truth," he said and rested his head back again. "I planned on torturing her for a long time." He looked out the side window then back into the rearview mirror. "I was gonna do it the same way I did that cop friend of yours who begged for his life. He kept rambling about his wife and kid and it just made me want to do it to him more. I could make three suffer instead of one. I have to tell you that it made his death that much sweeter. I decided I was going to get a little more creative and let it last awhile longer, but time wasn't on my side. I knew you guys were coming so I used a knife to the back and then the belly. Doing that doesn't excite me much anymore. I mean, the warm blood that covered my hands and the smell it gave off was great, and so are the sounds someone makes when they're dying. But there are so many ways to kill to make it exciting. I know the way I do it has to change because I've been doing it that way for so long."

Abernathy clamped his jaw down tight but didn't let go of the steering wheel. His heart hammered the inside of his chest, and his adrenaline soared. Every second of the drive he reconsidered visiting the idea of beating Dalton to an inch of his life. But he had his confession and closure recorded by an internal camera within the patrol car.

"On animals of course," Dalton said. "Your cop friend being my first human woke something up in me."

Abernathy calmed himself with the thought that the camera was the best thing that was ever installed in his cruiser. So was the fence between the front and back seats, which separated him from the criminals.

Abernathy punched a button on his dash and told the automated voice of his hands-free cell phone to call Bill Faulkner. He wanted to rub it in Dalton's face that he was found out, and he owed Bill the courtesy that he may have found officer Lenza's killer. Dirty play or not, Bill got it done, and Abernathy was thankful for it.

Abernathy also thought it best he give Bill free rein to post whatever he wanted. He would encourage it, in fact. It was time to start doing some good police work.

Chapter 20

BLOG ENTRY

Bill sat at his computer. While the old laptop loaded, he thought hard about what he was going to say. His hands shook with the news Abernathy had just given him. His head swam as he tried to comprehend how he had stood inches away from a sadistic killer and looked him in the eyes.

One of the girls said Schaeffer didn't have a soul. There wasn't one in Dalton either. He could sense that, and he was glad he hadn't dismissed what he felt. That would have been easy to do rather than telling Abernathy that he planted a recorder and putting himself out there for possible prosecution.

This Devil Tree was dirty business and seemed to drag the lowest society had to offer out from every crack they had been hidden in. He wondered what it was about that tree. He actually considered if it had anything to do with the tree at all. Maybe it had more to do with Schaeffer than a tree in the middle of a forest. But then how could Bill explain how the tree seemed to call out to him, too?

No longer wanting to contemplate about himself and the tree, he pressed his fingers into the keys and began to write his next blog entry.

The Devil Tree
There's Evil About

As you all know by now, a Port Saint Lucie officer was horrifically murdered at the Devil Tree. Stripped of his clothing, gutted, and hanged from the tree, suspicions of a satanic group began to surface in the law enforcement community because of the ritualistic type killing. The officer left behind a child and a wife.

I hope the madness around this tree stops. The lawlessness and cruelty that continues to play out there is because a sick serial killer chose that spot as his killing ground. Make no mistake about it: What he did was horrific, and it remains a stain on this good town.

Today I received news that it is becoming less of a suspicion that a satanic cult is at work and more of a probability.

An unidentified man has been taken into custody, and as my source (who will remain unnamed) explained, the prisoner has openly admitted to killing the officer at the tree.

The next steps are going to be an open nerve for us all. Now we have to wait for the police to interrogate the prisoner and see what sort of details surface. It is my hope to gain inside information about what transpires during the questioning. Let's hope they've found the imitation killer and that his arrest leads to anyone who might have helped him. Once the information becomes available, I will post it here.

Be diligent in making sure you report any suspicious activity to local authorities. Do not under any circumstance attempt to confront these people. They are extremely dangerous and are considered to be armed.

Bill Faulkner – staff writer

Chapter ②①

EVIL ABOUT

Abernathy stared at Dalton Vyle through the one-way mirror. Vyle sat in a hard steel chair and rested his forearms on the cold steel table that was screwed to the floor.

"Did you review the tape?" Abernathy said to Captain Brian Moore.

Captain Moore had his arms folded across his chest. "Reviewed and confirmed."

"So this is the son of a bitch who killed Lenza?"

"It sure sounded like that was what he said in many different ways."

Abernathy turned with start. "He admitted to killing Lenza. Why are we going through this?"

"His wording," the captain said. "It could be misconstrued by a defense attorney that he was talking about his intention to kill Bridget or even that he said what he did just to get a rise out of you."

"He gave details he couldn't possibly know without being the killer. That should be enough to lock him away for a long time."

Captain Moore clapped Abernathy's shoulder. "You know it's not. What he said doesn't prove anything. If he recants, we have nothing else to go on. I need you to put your feelings aside, and no matter what that creep in there says to you, I want you to maintain your composure at all times."

Abernathy nodded.

"I need you to get a full confession out of him."

"I'd rather just beat—"

"Don't say it," Captain Moore said. "I want you to stuff that down deep inside and get justice for Lenza and his family. That's what we need from you here and now. Let's put this creep away for a long time rather than getting him locked away for a few months on a minor assault charge. I want every 'I' dotted and every 'T' crossed."

Abernathy pushed everything down and turned away with determination. He carried a manila folder that had a sticker on the front: *Vyle, Dalton.* Abernathy arrived at the interrogation room door and drew a deep breath. He reached for the handle and noticed that his hand trembled. He had done hundreds, if not thousands of interrogations and he never had so much as a twitch. Scumbags were just scumbags, and it was his business to put them away. But he found this guy to be a different breed. He had killed Abernathy's friend and made no attempt to hide it. Maybe it wasn't just about Schaeffer and the tree. Maybe it had something to do with having been Schaeffer's ex-partner; being so close to that madness without ever knowing it.

Twisting the knob, he opened the door and looked at Dalton the entire time, from the moment he entered the room and shut the door until he sat down and placed his file on the tabletop.

"Bad cop again," Vyle said, an outward disposition of sarcasm all around him. Abernathy wanted to punch him in the face.

"This is getting old. I don't care how nice or mean you are to me. Laws are laws, and those are the parameters you have to work within, aren't they? That must be frustrating."

Abernathy knew he could get off a good ten to fifteen punches before his fellow officers reacted and got inside the room to pull him off the thug. But he took another deep breath, rested his elbows on the table, and looked into eyes independent of care and any connection to humanity.

"You come in here with your folder and your hard stare." Vyle laughed. "If you were someone I wanted, I would take you in your sleep or when you were looking right at me. It doesn't matter to me. Either way is fine."

"Did my colleague matter to you when you killed him?"

"No, he didn't matter. His life was all that I wanted for the tree."

"Why would you take a man's life for a goddamn tree?"

Dalton slapped the tabletop. "Goddamned it is."

"He was my friend."

"I don't care. Friends come and go."

Abernathy's hands curled into tight fists.

"Charge me and be done with it. I don't care. My purpose is to serve Baphomet. Stop wasting your breath by trying to pull something out of me that's just not there. I care nothing for your laws or your friends. I would kill them all if I had the chance."

"Baphomet," Abernathy whispered.

"Go to the tree and call his name. He will come."

Abernathy picked up Dalton's file, tapped it on the table, and held it to his chest. "Never . . . just like you will never get the chance to do what you did again."

"I served as I was supposed to, but there are so many more."

"How many," Abernathy asked. "How many more of you are there?"

Dalton's lips turned up into a satisfied smile. "We are Legion, and we are many."

"Why kill officer Lenza?"

"Because I could."

"Why did you want to kill Bridget?"

"Because Schaeffer heard the calling but was unable to complete the task. We are ready to finish his work . . . to satisfy the tree and Baphomet."

"I'm glad you'll never see outside the confines of the cold brick walls that'll contain you. You are an animal," Abernathy said and left the interrogation room. He went in to see Captain Moore, who still stared at Dalton through the one-way mirror.

"Good job," the captain said. "Now we also know he wasn't acting alone."

"That's little consolation. If I was able to catch them before they did what they did to Lenza, then it would have been a good job."

"Breck told me you were being hard on yourself. You are a good cop. You pulled out important information we can use to our advantage."

"How so?"

"He told us there are more. We can get them."

"And I know how. We can make it seem like we believe Dalton acted alone. We can let that slip out into the media." Abernathy looked at Dalton and then looked at the captain. "Do you trust me to do the right thing with this case, Captain?"

"Of course I do."

"Thank you. Now, if you'll excuse me, I have some work to do."

The captain nodded and Abernathy walked away, pulling out his cell phone as he moved forward with determination. He went into a private room and called Bill Faulkner.

"Bill?"

"Hello, Officer Abernathy."

"I just interrogated Dalton, and I wanted to confirm what I said to you earlier. The lead you provided resulted in the arrest of officer Lenza's killer. You did excellent journalistic work, and for that I owe you."

"You don't owe me anything."

"Listen. We found a circular clearing in the woods just behind the tree. The mattresses that were in this clearing were covered in Lenza's blood. We believe the cult had an orgy in his blood after they killed him."

"These people are sick bastards."

"That's an understatement. There's a killer cult out there, but we don't want to let them know we know about it. Please make another blog entry simply saying the killer was caught and that he acted alone. Tell the town they can breathe a sigh of relief."

"I can do that. I want these people caught. I'm concerned for my safety and that of so many others."

"By playing dumb to their existence we will draw them out. We are going to start preparing to move on them."

"I'll make the blog post right now."

"Thank you, Bill, I appreciate that. Also, he admitted that they had chosen Bridget to be the next victim of the tree because Schaeffer failed to give it what it wanted. He claimed that she is what it wanted, and they were going to give her to it."

"Do you think she needs protection?"

"I'll be setting that up as soon as we hang up the phone. I should have a detail on her within a half hour. I'm going to assign them to her twenty-four/seven for the next couple weeks. I'll even offer for her to come here, where she can be placed into protective custody."

"That's good," Bill said. "That woman has been through enough."

"Yes," Abernathy said, and his voice trailed off. "Yes she has."

"Don't forget about Elizabeth."

"I didn't. I'm going to send Breck to get her."

"OK. Let me hang up so I can write the blog entry and you can get to protecting the girls."

BLOG ENTRY

Bill hung up his phone and immediately accessed his blog. The post he had made only an hour ago had thousands of hits already. People were paying attention, and he needed to get Abernathy's message out there immediately. He started to type, and the words flowed like his still insatiable desire to be around the tree.

The Devil Tree
Officer Lenza's Killer Caught

Confirmation came in the way of an anonymous tip from someone very close to the case. It is verified that the killer of Officer Lenza is in custody and has been placed under arrest.

What does this mean for Port Saint Lucie?

I think we can take a deep breath and exhale knowing our streets and park are safer. Now maybe the ancient oak tree—which I will no longer refer to as the Devil Tree—can finally reside quietly in the patch of forest it has stood in for over a century.

Maybe time can dull the stain left behind and people can forget what has happened there. I propose a challenge to everyone reading this blog entry. I ask that you use Oak Hammock Park as a place of peace and pleasant recreation, and don't pass the C-24 sign in search of the tree. Do that out of respect for Officer Lenza and his family. Let the tree fade into the background of our everyday life, and let's find comfort in knowing that the police have done a fine job in catching the killer so quickly.

The killer has admitted to working alone and explained what he had done in great detail, leaving no question that he is indeed the killer. He stated that his actions were made to look like there were many involved—a tactic I will admit had me fooled and on edge. I'm certain it had a lot of us worried. But hearing the relief in my source's voice has given me peace of mind, and I hope what I've written does the same for you.

Bill Faulkner – staff writer

Bill hit the post button, sat back in his chair, and thought about his conversation with Abernathy. He couldn't help but focus on the idea that it might take up to a half an hour to get someone on the detail to protect Bridget.

He didn't want to interfere with what Abernathy was doing, but he needed to make sure she was all right. That something-isn't-right feeling was nagging at him again, and it couldn't be ignored. He needed to check on her and make sure she was safe.

Chapter ②③

BRIDGET

Bridget sat on her couch and continued to ponder what had happened just a little while ago with Dalton and Officer Abernathy. Having just read Bill Faulkner's blog post, she couldn't believe she was walking around a sadistic killer in her own house and didn't know it. There was no doubt in her mind that he wanted to take her to that damn tree and try to reenact what Schaeffer had planned to do to her.

Abernathy and Bill Faulkner didn't need to spell that out for her. She was no dummy, and now that she looked at it for what it was, it was obvious. No matter what she told her friends, Dalton wasn't there to protect her or check in on her. He came right after the Schaeffer incident and was cunning enough to wiggle his way in and gain her trust. He was there to kidnap her, take her away, and do unspeakable things to her.

The thought of calling Elizabeth and telling her everything that just happened crossed her mind. She went for her phone when a gentle knock at the door sidetracked her.

"That was quick," she said aloud to herself and put her phone away.

Officer Abernathy had called not too long ago and said he would be coming over or sending another officer within a half hour.

"Don't bother packing anything," Abernathy had said on the phone. "We're going to watch you at your house and have a detail outside, but we thought it safer to move you until this is over. We will provide anything you might need."

"OK," she had said, and that's when she settled on the couch and contemplated the decisions she'd made that didn't really make much sense to her.

She grabbed her purse and made sure she had her keys as she went to the front door. After she was safe in Abernathy's custody, she would ask him to pick up Elizabeth, too. Even though she was fairly certain they had already made arrangements to do that, she was concerned for her friend nevertheless. If they were after her, then there was no doubt they would go after Elizabeth as well.

According to Abernathy, they seemed more fixated on her, however, because she was the one who had actually foiled Schaeffer's plans. Although she had successfully maneuvered their escape from Schaeffer himself, now it seemed their very escape from the killer and the Devil Tree would be their curse.

She shook that thought and opened the door with a smile and a feeling of being safe. Before she could register what she was looking at, two faceless people charged into the house and knocked her over, slamming her to the ground. Her back hit first, and then her head bounced off the hardwood floor. Dazed, blackness threatened to overtake her consciousness as her world went out of focus. Her sense of what to do to protect herself was lost amidst the initial blow to the head.

"Your karate ain't gonna do you no good, bitch," one of them said, and she felt a fist cross her jaw several times as blackness filled her head again. Her consciousness came in and out in waves of pain and was accompanied with the taste of blood. Her mouth filled up and she wanted to spit it out, but it filled the back of her throat instead and she began to choke.

"Quick, flip her over and get her arms behind her back," another said.

Her ears rang, and as hard as she tried to get herself together, she just couldn't get her bearings.

"For we are Legion and we are many. You cannot fight us. We will have you hanging from that tree, but first you will beg for your life."

"We want you to admit that your life has been a waste since you escaped Schaeffer. That it had no meaning since his sacrifice. But that will happen when you return to the tree. You will have your chance."

She was rolled over onto her belly, and the blood poured out of her mouth in thick gobs. There was no fight left in her. Her attackers were strong and were smart enough to keep her dazed by hitting her hard and often so that her ability to recover from the assault would be impossible.

Her arms were forced behind her back, and they zip-tied her wrists together and pulled the hard plastic tight, cutting off the circulation. They did the same thing to her ankles and then pulled a sack over her head. A final blow she couldn't possibly see coming smashed into her cheekbone, and along with the rattling clunk that filled her head, a wave of blackness came over her completely. Strangely, her final thoughts before blacking out were about the tasks she wanted to get done today and now wouldn't have the chance to complete. Maybe she would never get to do them ever.

Chapter 20

QUICK THINKING

Bill hurried to Bridget's house, ignoring stop signs and red lights. Pushing the small engine on his beat up Volkswagen Bug as hard as he could, he had an overwhelming feeling that Dalton Vyle was merely a distraction and that Abernathy may have overlooked the severity behind the threat he posed once they removed him. The cult wanted to get to Bridget, and the thought that Vyle was merely a pawn to get it done . . . made to throw the police off? He couldn't finish the thought in his desperate effort to save her.

Bill arrived at Bridget's house and slammed on the brakes. The tires squealed, and in one fluid movement, he exited the vehicle and ran to the front door. He knocked hard and paced back and forth.

"Come on, come on," he said and pulled his cell phone out of his pocket. He looked at the time and decided he was giving her thirty seconds to get to the door before he kicked it down.

"Ah, screw it," he said and he tried the handle, expecting it to be locked. To his surprise, it turned. He pushed the door open, and as it swung back it revealed furniture that had been knocked

over and an area rug that was bunched up and pushed aside. A
large pool of blood stained the floor, indicating that a fierce battle
had broken out in the living room.

He stepped away and closed the door. His hands shook, but he
managed to dial Abernathy using voice commands on his
smartphone.

"Yeah, Bill?"

"I just got to Bridget's house—I just had to see for myself that
she was OK until you guys arrived. The door was unlocked. When
I looked inside I could see some of the furniture had been knocked
over. The rug is all bunched up, and there's blood on the floor. It's
a lot of blood. I think they got her."

"Have you checked the house?"

"No, I didn't think I should. I didn't break the threshold of the
doorway because I didn't want to contaminate the crime scene."

"Good job, Bill," Abernathy said. "I never thought they'd act
this quickly and in broad daylight. They're getting brazen and
seem to have a plan." Abernathy sighed. "I didn't see this one
coming."

Bill looked down the street both ways and he didn't see
anyone. "Maybe the neighbors should be questioned. They might
have seen something that can help us get to her."

"We will do that, but for now I want you to go home. Stay there
until you hear from me. I may need you before this is over."

"I don't mean to tell you how to do your job, but I think your
concern should shift to Elizabeth. If they came to get Bridget to do
whatever they're planning, I'm sure they'll go after Elizabeth, too.
They'll need her to complete their plan. Schaeffer intended to kill
them both, and from what we know, it only makes sense that both
girls are targets."

"I agree, Bill, and good work; every second counts. Breck is on his way to Elizabeth's house, and I'll keep you posted. We will get Bridget back. I promise not to have anyone else's blood on my hands. I'm going to stop these bastards no matter what."

Bill heard a man who meant business and then a dial tone.

Chapter ②⑤

ELIZABETH

Breck arrived at Elizabeth's apartment, and he hurried to the door. Making sure he was heard, he knocked with a heavy hand and stepped back. Looking all around the neighborhood and back at the door, he rested his hand on his gun.

The locks on the door clicked, and Elizabeth opened the door.

"Oh," she said and took a nervous step backwards.

"Elizabeth Brown?"

"That's right."

"I'm Officer Breck," he said and clicked the button on his radio. "Ten-twenty-five, I'm in contact with subject."

"Ten-four," dispatch responded.

"I'll see if I can get her to come along, dispatch."

"Ten-two." The radio chirped.

"What's going on?" Elizabeth said, still well inside the door.

Breck looked at Elizabeth and peered into the apartment around her. He soon focused his eyes on her. "Has anyone tried to contact you or have you noticed anyone unfamiliar around your complex over the last few days?"

"No," Elizabeth said and shrank back. "Why? What's going on? You're scaring me."

"Your friend, Bridget, was abducted from her house just a little while ago, and we believe it was by members of the cult who have been at the tree. We believe the threat is geared toward you as well."

"Are you sure she was abducted? I mean she goes to the gym and dojo all the time."

"I'm sure, Ms. Brown. We believe it has something to do with the body you two found at the tree. An officer was murdered at the tree a few nights ago, and as I just mentioned, we believe there is a cult involved. Your safety is our number one concern right now, and we believe you are in immediate danger."

"Are you saying they're after me?"

"Yes, ma'am, that is exactly what I'm saying."

"What would they want with me?" Her eyes welled with tears. The fear she felt clearly rattled her entire body. "Why would they take Bridget? What do they want with her? She's never done anything to anyone!"

"I know. We are not one hundred percent sure, but we think they're trying to finish what Schaeffer started. You two were the only ones to escape him and ultimately exposed what he was doing. That's going to make you both top targets." Breck adjusted his vest as Elizabeth whimpered. "I think you should come with me so we can protect you and figure things out back at the precinct. Maybe there are things you can tell us about your friend. Any clues you provide might help us find her."

"They couldn't have gotten her," Elizabeth said. "She's a second degree black belt in karate—maybe even a third degree. She's aware of her surroundings and is really tough."

"I don't want to get into the details here, ma'am. Get only the basics of what you need and come with me."

"OK," Elizabeth said and walked around the apartment, indecisively and without purpose.

"Ma'am?"

Elizabeth stopped and looked at Breck.

"Get your pocketbook and keys. That's all you'll need. Anything else we can get for you later."

She nodded. "OK." She started picking up things around the apartment.

Breck watched her for a moment before he stepped inside. "Elizabeth?"

She stopped.

"I'm here to help you. Do you understand what I'm telling you?"

"Yes. No." She began to cry. "There is no way they can keep her captive. She's tougher than most men I know." Elizabeth plopped down on the couch and cradled her face in her hands. "This can't be happening."

Breck knelt in front of her. "I'm sorry you have to go through this, but we need to move. The more time we spend here, the further away our chance of recovering her quickly becomes."

Elizabeth picked at her fingernails. "I don't want to go."

"Elizabeth, I strongly suggest you reconsider what you're saying."

"I can't be there," she said with bright red eyes. "There's nothing I can tell you about Bridget that you don't already know. She's just a regular girl who keeps to herself. I want to go to my half sister's house. She lives about an hour south in West Palm Beach."

"We could use your help learning about your friend."

"I can't do this," Elizabeth said. Her shoulders sagged and she sobbed uncontrollably. "Even though she's really quiet, she's tough. She saved my life. That's all there is to know about her. If she gets a chance, she'll kick all their asses and get away."

"I still would like you to come with me. I'm concerned about your safety."

Elizabeth shook her head. "No offense, but one of the last interactions I had with a cop almost got Bridget and me killed. I'm going to go to my sister's. I'll be better off going there."

"OK," Breck said. "I won't pressure you anymore. If you think your sister's place is a safe place for you to be, then I think that's where you should go."

"I want to grab some clothes," she said. "And I don't want to forget my pocketbook." She got up and started moving from room to room gathering things.

"I'd like to offer to take you to the precinct one last time. Are you sure you won't reconsider coming with me? We can watch over you. Protect you."

"I'm sure," Elizabeth said. "I have to get away from here. That stupid tree has cost me enough, and now it may have cost me my best friend. I don't even know what to think anymore."

"We don't know that, and like you said, she's tough."

"Where do you think they took her?"

"We don't know. We're trying to figure that out."

"I'm going to my sister's house. She has a different last name than me and lives far enough away from here that no one will know where I am."

Breck looked Elizabeth in the eyes. "Be safe, Ms. Brown, and be aware of everything around you. If something doesn't seem right, get to a safe place and call the police."

She nodded with an armful of clothes. "OK."

Breck exited the apartment and stood on the porch. Elizabeth put down what she held. "I'm going to pack a small suitcase." She disappeared farther into her home.

Breck walked the outside perimeter of the apartment complex with a watchful eye and then looked over everything again with a meticulous eye. When he saw all was clear, he got into his car, picked up his radio, and held the button.

"I've located her, but she's refusing to come in. Ten-forty-eight," Breck said.

"Ten-four."

"She wants to stay at a relative's house in West Palm Beach. I'm going to stay and make sure she gets in her car and out of here safely."

"Ten-four."

Elizabeth exited her apartment and locked the door behind her. She piled her things into a red Mini Cooper and drove away. Breck followed her for several blocks, and when she got onto US-1, he broke away and returned to the precinct.

Chapter 26

IN A HOLE

Bridget began to stir. Her head pounded and her right eye was swollen shut and her jaw dangled open and felt like it was dislocated. She tried to open her mouth and winced. With her tongue she could feel the jagged teeth that were cracked and the spaces where they had been shattered.

She realized her plastic cuffs had been cut off, and she rubbed her cheek with a gentle touch; the feeling was muted by the extreme swelling that felt like a rock underneath her skin.

Whoever it was who had hit her packed a mean right hook. If she had seen it coming she might have been able to defend herself. But the way they charged in and used surprise to their advantage, she didn't stand a chance. It wasn't so much being charged, but when her head bounced off the hard floor and that was followed up with a hard punch, she was too thrown off to retaliate. They knew about her karate background and made sure they neutralized her immediately.

She had to give them credit: Smart play on their part.

The room she found herself confined in was dark, musty, and even a bit chilly. A sliver of light beamed down from above her, and she could see she was in a rectangular hole dug deep into the earth. She was at least ten feet down, and the ceiling above her was far too high for her to reach. There was some sort of slab or plywood being used as a covering, and it was in the dead center of the room, keeping her from being able to use the side walls to her advantage.

She was being teased by the only entrance and exit. The only way out, it seemed, would be from the use of a ladder—which she didn't have.

As she looked around, she realized that there was nothing in the small prison but her and the four confining walls and a smell of dirt. She rested her back against the wall and brought her knees to her chest. Her wrists had brush burns on them, and she noticed her ankles had the same marks as well. The raw skin oozed, and dirt clung to it like it was glue.

She tried to forget about her injuries and focus on only serious thoughts that might help her out of this situation. As she hugged her legs, ideas started to whirl around her head. Most people would panic and not use this valuable time to try to formulate a plan, she acknowledged. She needed to make sure that's exactly what she was doing.

"I am no victim," she reminded herself aloud and thought about the tree. "I beat you once. I want you to know I'm going to beat you again."

Whatever she could come up with would be better than just sitting here and worrying about her injuries, she decided. She sensed the certainty of a time limit, which was impossible to ignore. Once the sun went down, they would come for her and she would be used as a sacrifice to the tree. If they didn't come this night, then it would most likely be the next. She was sure of it.

No matter her training, she understood that they were going to come in numbers and she wouldn't stand a chance against a mob. Fighting her way out of this wasn't an option. Her best bet was to try to escape before they came for her.

Maybe she could use her hands to dig at the dirt and make a large pile beneath the slab overhead that would allow her to reach it and climb her way out. Once she was out, she would make a run for it. She doubted anyone could match her stamina—even in the condition she was in.

Pushing herself to her feet, she used stiff fingers to try to rake through the soil. The firmly packed dirt was like scraping her fingers against rock. She pushed harder, but the earth broke her fingernails and ripped her skin. Her strength had dwindled greatly from the barbaric attack, and she settled on her haunches, short of breath.

Although the idea was great, the execution, it seemed, was nothing short of impossible. Even if she had the strength to dig, the process of piling the dirt high enough to get her to the height of the hatch would take her hours. She didn't have the strength or the time.

"I'm not thinking clearly," she said, and her voice echoed around the small dirt room.

She stood underneath the covering overhead and looked into the gap. She could see branches and leaves and a blue sky. Surrounding her mouth with her hands, she got onto her toes, drew a deep breath, and shouted, "Help! Someone help me! I'm down here!"

Her lips were fat and split, and her scream made her recoil from the shot of pain. The call sounded hollow and only annoyed the steady ache in her face and head. It was doubtful this hole was anywhere near people, and screaming was far too painful and a waste of energy.

While she was unsure how long she had been out, she did know that as time went on she would only get weaker from her untreated injuries. That also meant she would become less likely to be able to fend off her attackers, even if they came in lower numbers and in disorder. She wasn't fooling anyone; she was merely trying to keep herself away from the fear that was closing in around her. They knew what she was capable of, and they wouldn't give her a chance.

"I'm going to die for a tree," she said and sat down to try to conserve some energy. "I'm going to die for a fucking tree. They already know that I'm able to defend myself. There's only one thing I can do." She bowed her head. "I'm going to pick one and take that prick down with me. These fucking people . . . I hate them all."

STRATEGY

Breck sat on the corner of the desk, and Abernathy stood next to him with his arms folded.

"What is it, Abernathy?" Captain Moore said and took a sip of coffee out of an insulated cup.

"Schaeffer and this tree . . . it just won't go away."

No one said a thing because what Abernathy said was true.

"I stood next to Schaeffer and didn't even have a clue. When we were looking at the bones in the ground, searching around the tree and considering all the markings, he was really mocking me. He did all those things and acted like it was all a big surprise. And I moved around, revealing tiny pieces of evidence or clues he left behind. He knew whether or not I was close to him."

Abernathy shook his head.

"Yes, he was your partner, but you did your best, and he mocked us all," Captain Moore said. "Not just you. He was doing it right underneath all of our noses, and we were none the wiser. Not a single one of us."

Abernathy sighed. "And now we have this cult—clan, group, or whatever the hell you want to call them—trying to carry out his plan and finish what he started." Abernathy stopped pulling at his chin and let his hands fall at his sides. "How do they think they're going to take this girl to the tree and kill her?"

"I don't think they will," Breck said.

"They know we're going to be crawling all over there like ants on a mound," the captain said.

"But what happens if we don't go to the tree?" Breck said.

Captain Moore shook his head. "Excuse me? We can guess that these people aren't stupid enough to try to take her to the tree and use her as their next sacrifice tonight."

"No," Abernathy said. "I think Breck is onto something. I think they might wait and see if there is a presence at the tree. I think they're smart enough to wait things out. I'm sure they're going to be careful and see how legit Bill's blog post is. That was my mole; my play at trying to get them to come out of the shadows."

Captain Moore rocked on his feet. "I don't think we should chance leaving that park unoccupied. I don't like it."

"I don't either," Abernathy said. "On that we agree. We already lost one of our own there, and we have to play this smart."

"Go ahead, boys, tell me what you're thinking," the captain said.

"Maybe we should have patrol roll through," Breck said. "Two people in the car, just in case, and to show them we've beefed up protection of our own people."

Abernathy nodded. "They can do a pass by and maybe even get out and check the grounds by the tree a few times. We should instruct them that they're not to look too hard. Maybe make it a quick pass in and out of the park. Have them make small talk about how quiet everything is."

"OK, now tell me the rest here. I need something I can chew on, boys," Captain Moore said.

"I'm certain they're going to have someone there—if they're not there already," Breck said. "If I were a betting man, I'd say they probably covered their spy in leaves somewhere deep in a thicket. Who knows, I wouldn't put it past them to have on ghillie suits and night vision goggles."

"I'm sure if the person who's been planted to stake out the area doesn't come back, Bridget is as good as dead no matter where she is," Abernathy said. "We've got to let this person see and hear what's going on. We don't find him no matter what."

"If there is a someone for us not to find." Captain Moore paused, evidently contemplating, and took another sip from his coffee cup. "That's an interesting approach that I might be willing to gamble on. Maybe they'll believe we think we caught the killer with this Dalton Vyle and that he was able to keep his mouth shut and convince us he acted alone."

Abernathy and Breck nodded. "That's what we had Bill the Blogger put out there. It is a gamble, but I had him release that information with the hopes of this scenario playing out," Abernathy said.

"All right," the captain continued. "We don't put anything out there on the missing girl and make sure the lid stays locked tight on that. If we act like we don't even know she's missing—"

"They'll be sure to act," Abernathy said. "I know it."

"Exactly," the captain said.

"I'm going to go back to my original idea and suggesting that we don't even pass through the park the entire night," Breck said. "If we do go through we cut it off at like one or two a.m." Breck took a moment. "I think three a.m. is dead time or some shit like that. I heard that's like their witching hour or something."

Captain Moore worked on his coffee some more, and his eyes bounced back and forth between his two officers. Abernathy began to pace with his hands on his hips. It was Breck's turn to watch them both. The tension was thick, and indecision hung in the air like a heavy blanket. It was a risky call, but the captain had to decide.

"I can't figure where they might have her," Abernathy said. "I've been racking my brain since we knew she was gone."

"I think one of them has her with them," Breck said.

Abernathy shook his head. "No. They have her locked away somewhere. Bridget is far too dangerous to leave with one person, and she remains a threat to them so as long as she's still alive."

"Do you think she's alive?" Breck said.

Abernathy stared. "I don't want to think any differently, and we can't approach this from any other way yet."

Captain Moore sighed. "Breck . . ."

"No, he has a legitimate question," Abernathy said. "One I thought myself, but I didn't want to be the one to say so. I've been trying to keep that thought out of my head, but I suppose we have to address it."

"So . . . if she's dead?" Captain Moore said. "What are you thinking?"

"I'm thinking there is no way they killed her because that means they didn't fulfill their plan to finish what Schaeffer started. That's what this is all about, and it has to be done at the tree," Abernathy said.

"And if she was already dead I'm sure we would have found her hanging from that tree or found her body discarded already," Breck said.

"Post mortem, as stiff as a board, and desecrated," Abernathy said. "There will be a pissed off group of people looking for the other girl who was involved, too."

"She's in Palm Beach County with a relative," Breck said.

"Who did she say she was going to stay with?"

"She said a half sister or something. She was really frantic and was changing her mind every two seconds. She was visibly upset and just wanted to get away from the tree and those people and she doesn't trust the police. I checked the surrounding area because I thought there might be someone there influencing her. But everything was clear, and I escorted her all the way to US-1."

"I can't say I blame her for bugging out and not trusting the police," Abernathy said. "We will have to be ready to move on her quickly if this doesn't work. Maybe we can get someone working on who she went to stay with."

The captain nodded. "I'll get the ball rolling on that."

"And the officers who are assigned to visiting that tree later need specific instructions and have to play this exactly as we discussed."

"They will," Captain Moore said. "They'll do exactly as they're supposed to. I'm personally taking responsibility for these ladies. I don't want anything happening to either of them. Do you hear me?"

"Loud and clear. We'll get her back," Abernathy said. "We're smarter than them, and we know we all have our parts to play. We are not giving that tree another body. Never again."

"So what's the plan after we do this tonight?"

"We set a trap and get them tomorrow night. That's when I believe they will move. I want this self-proclaimed Legion dismantled top to bottom and to recover Bridget alive," Abernathy said. "That's our goal and collective focus." Abernathy's cell phone rang, and he saw it was Bill. "Excuse me," he said. "I've got to take this, but it seems like everything we've discussed here is settled."

"It is settled. That is how we are going to proceed," the captain said, and Breck reiterated the plan as Abernathy stepped out of the room to take the call.

"Hello, Bill, what do you have?"

Chapter 28

EVERYTHING IS A STORY

Bill had parked his car down the street from Elizabeth's house and was relying on his reporter instinct to get to the bottom of what was really going on. In his mind, the dots weren't connecting, and there was a story here that needed to be discovered. As of right now, he needed to remain on the sidelines and allow this thing to play out.

He had used trees, parked cars, and shrubbery as cover as he watched Officer Breck pull away with Elizabeth almost fifteen minutes ago. It was no surprise when she returned home about five minutes ago and disappeared into her house. That was the intuition he had. He knew he was onto something, but what it was, exactly, eluded him for the moment. The fact that Elizabeth hadn't stayed away confused and intrigued him. What was really going on here?

His heart beat hard and he had to pee in the worst way. But he forgot all that when a loud, white Chevy Camaro pulled into her driveway and Elizabeth came outside with her handbag and hurried into the car. It backed out of the driveway and slowly made its way down the street.

Bill watched with unwavering curiosity and recited the license plate number to himself until he grabbed a pen and paper to write it down. He wanted to make sure he had all the information to pass over to Abernathy. While it was fresh on his mind, he wrote down the make and color of the vehicle and wrote the license plate number.

He called Abernathy, who picked up on the second ring.

"Abernathy," the voice came through the phone.

"It's Bill. I parked down the block from Elizabeth's house after I left Bridget's house, and I saw Breck there for a while. I hid behind cars and stuff so they wouldn't make me."

"Yeah, Breck said she didn't want to go with him and left for a sister's house or something in Palm Beach. Breck is back here with me."

"Well, she didn't really leave."

"What do you mean?"

"She came back home."

"Go on."

"A white Camaro just pulled up about thirty seconds ago and picked her up," Bill said. "I couldn't see who was driving because the windows were tinted. I thought it worth the effort for you to run the plate."

"You're going to get a badge before this is over."

Bill chuckled. "I just want Bridget and Elizabeth to be safe and to get these people off the streets."

"OK, what is it?"

"AC3B4F. Florida plate."

"Hang on a second," Abernathy said and Bill could hear him hold the phone away from his ear. "Hey, Breck, run this plate and let me know who it belongs to."

Abernathy came back on the line. "It'll take just a minute here."

"OK," Bill said, but he couldn't shake the feeling that her coming home and this person coming to pick her up wasn't right. He had covered too many stories, followed too many leads to know when things weren't adding up. What he just saw made no sense at all. Why would she leave and then come back? Was she pretending to shake Breck?

"The vehicle belongs to a Travis Kidwell," Abernathy said. "He lives in West Palm Beach."

"What does that mean?" Bill said.

"Nothing at this point. Elizabeth told Breck she was going to spend time with family down there." Abernathy breathed into the phone. "He was probably some friend that was asked to pick her up and drive her down there. Maybe she was too shaken up to drive or something. I don't know."

Bill shook his head. The feeling not leaving his investigative mind meant that things weren't right. "Do you have any record on this guy at all?"

"No, he's clean."

Bill slouched and exhaled. "I can't explain how wrong that feels to me."

"I'll see if we can get the captain to send someone out from the Palm Beach PD to check on her."

"Sooner than later?"

"Yes, I'm going to get it in motion as soon as we hang up. There will be no hesitations this time, Bill. They will get to the house right around the time Elizabeth and Mr. Kidwell should be arriving or very soon after. I'll call you."

"OK, thank you. I don't want to keep you then. I know you have a lot of work to do," Bill said and hung up the phone. Disappointment that they didn't come back with a hit on Travis Kidwell filled Bill with conflict. He had this right. He knew it. It was a rare occurrence that he would get the feeling to follow leads around this closely and run into a dead end. Maybe he would do some digging when he got home while he was waiting for Abernathy to call him back. He'd do a search on this Mr. Kidwell and see what he could unearth.

Bill tucked his notepad into his pocket and made his way back to his Volkswagen Bug. His search for truth was motivated by his feeling that things were not right. His recourse was limited only by his approach, and he had a million of those tucked away and ready to use.

It was time to pull out all the stops for the sake of the women's well-being.

Chapter ②⑨

SHOCKING NEWS

Bill sat at the table in the kitchen and drummed his fingers on the wooden top. Knowing this was where they found Susan's body and that she had seemed to stick around, he felt obligated to talk to her.

"That tree is no good," he said. "I know you know that because look at what it turned Jim into."

The house was quiet, but Bill wanted a response. Provoking was a way to get one, he'd heard, and wanted to see if it worked. "Is this where he strangled you?"

Bill listened to the house for a long while but didn't hear a thing.

"Did you feel any pain?"

Still the house remained quiet. Although his attempted conversation with the dead woman was a good distraction, his mind returned to the tree and the bizarre events that had surrounded it ever since he heard about it.

Bodies were discovered by a local fisherman and the local authorities had exhumed the dead. They realized the corpses were of a male and female who had been murdered a year before and were buried beneath the tree.

Jim became a suspect and spoke about how the tree was commanding him to act strangely. Soon after he snapped, he attacked Officer Abernathy, knocking him out, and then killed his own wife. Soon it was discovered that Officer Schaeffer was the killer and a known satanist.

While he ran amok killing people, his last attempt at getting a sacrifice for the tree ended in disaster for him. He'd kidnapped two women and made a mistake in his selection and his ability to keep them under his control.

After a struggle ensued between him and the two women, they escaped and were able to identify him as the killer, oddly enough, at the police precinct where he served as a sheriff's deputy. His picture had been on the wall and the women easily identified him.

"Everything about this tree and what Schaeffer did there is bad news," Bill said, no longer interested in taunting Susan. "I'm sorry about what I said to you. I'm desperate for someone to talk to. I can't help but think how once you've been exposed to the tree it's like you've walked underneath a ladder or a black cat has crossed your path. The tree attracts bad people with very bad intentions, and it seems that whatever it gets is never enough. I say that because this time it called forth a devil-worshiping clan that I never thought in a million years existed here in Port Saint Lucie." He shook his head and stood. "No blog entry this time, I'm afraid. I'm leaving again so the house is all yours. I'm going to see Jim to see if he has anything else he needs to tell me. If that pisses you off, maybe you should open some cabinets and tip some things over so I know you're here and you can hear my words." He laughed. "I know you won't because it's probably all in my head. But if you are here, I'm just making a suggestion. At least then I'll know for sure it's you. Do you hear me?" He looked around the small kitchen and even eyed the pantry closet. "I know what Jim is going to tell me. He's going to say to stay away from the tree, to let the police handle what is going on. He was the first to warn everyone of a malevolent presence connected to that tree. I know he could use the visit. Is there anything you'd like me tell him while I'm there?"

The house remained quiet enough that he could hear the beat of his own heart. He wondered if Susan could only draw energy at nighttime.

"I'll let you know what he says when I get back," Bill said. He grabbed his keys from the hook on the wall and walked out the front door.

Bill arrived at Port Saint Lucie Prison and went to the visitor desk.

"I'm here to see Jim Perry," he said and slid his driver's license across the desk.

"You're that reporter who helped break the Schaeffer case."

"I am," Bill said. "I am currently working closely with Officer Abernathy and some of the other officers on what's been happening with the tree. I don't know if you've heard, but activity has picked up at the tree again."

"I know," the female officer said, and her face exhibited the sadness of having lost someone she knew. "Word spreads fast in the law enforcement community when one of our own loses their life."

"I'm sorry. I shouldn't have said that. It was very presumptuous of me to think otherwise. Of course you know."

"That's OK. It was innocent conversation," she said and typed on a computer. Her facial expression showed shock. She slid the license back toward Bill. "I'm sorry, it seems not everything travels so quickly through our grapevine. I regret to inform you that Mr. Perry committed suicide last night."

Bill stood there, sharing in her surprise, the news like an unblocked slap to the face. He tried to maintain his composure and remember to breathe. "Ha—how?"

"It doesn't give details here. You'd have to file a request with records."

"Damn it."

"Yes, it's a tragedy, really. All of the officers here liked to talk to Mr. Perry. They gained a lot of insight on that tree because of him." She laughed. "Sorry, it's just something I'm recalling. It wasn't easy for the guards to get things out of Jim. But they quickly found out when they offered him extra amenities he'd share a bunch, but he was smart enough to never reveal everything he knew."

"What about his daughter?"

"Says here that next of kin has already been informed."

Bill shook his head. "His death is a shame. I thought he was a nice man plagued with something unexplainable," Bill said. "I don't know how he did it, but knowing what he went through and his state of mind, I think he should have been monitored a little closer."

"At least he had a visitor from his family member earlier in the day."

"His daughter came here?" Bill's eyes lit up with the idea of getting Jim's last words out of her. Maybe he would be able to make peace with whatever it was he had said to her. There was guilt hidden deep that Bill coming to see Jim had somehow caused him to react the way he did. Maybe he didn't want to talk about the tree at all and it pushed him over the edge.

"No," the female officer said. "It was his daughter's son. He lives locally. I know that because I was the one who checked him in."

"Do you know his name? Maybe have an address?"

"I know his name," she said and rested her elbows on the desk. "The name was so unique to me that I actually remember it without having to look it up."

"Do you mind providing me with a little inside information?"

"Travis," she said, and for Bill, time started to crawl as he waited to hear the last name. "His name is Travis Kidwell."

Bill's flesh goosed. "Travis Kidwell? Are you sure?"

"I'm as positive as you're standing right here in front of me."

Bill thought about that for a moment but didn't know what the connection was. This guy visited Jim yesterday, Jim killed himself, and then this guy picked up Elizabeth today. Did Jim's actions have anything to do with Travis? Maybe he reported news to him that Jim couldn't bear. Was he told about Officer Lenza being dismembered, and he could no longer stand the curse of the tree?

"OK, thank you," Bill said. His mouth was dry, and his head swam with the news. "I'm going to let Officer Abernathy know because he's following a lead on him already. We didn't know he was related to Jim."

"That's fine, just don't say you heard it from me," the female officer said. "Use that term 'anonymous source' you're so fond of."

"OK, and I will."

"Thank you."

Bill staggered out of the prison, using the wall to help guide him. He needed to gather himself before he could call Abernathy.

Bill exited his Volkswagen Bug and leaned against it while he thought. His heart was heavy, and he contended with a bit of anger he didn't care to acknowledge. This tree was becoming more of a problem than it was worth and had taken more lives than he cared to know. It was nonsense that the damn thing couldn't be cut down, burned, or just simply uprooted.

He walked around the back of the house and looked inside the shed. Although he had been in the house for just about six months, this was the first time he had even ventured into the back yard.

The old dilapidated storage shed was in the same condition the house was in. Maybe one day, when all this craziness blew over, he would get to fixing things. That would be a great distraction and a great use of his spare time when he wasn't freelancing, he thought.

The door was padlocked, and out of frustration Bill grabbed the handle and pulled as hard as he could. The hasp broke away from the rotted wood, and the door swung open.

Miscellaneous supplies filled the small shed, and he saw an ax hanging on the wall, a gas can sitting on the floor, and a very old chainsaw sopped in oil and caked with sawdust on a bench. The chainsaw was a Stihl 026; a very reliable and powerful saw.

He took the gasoline and chainsaw out and found bar oil, too. He checked the gas and oil reservoirs and they were still full. There was a possibility the gasoline may have gone stale so he would have to test its worthiness.

Setting the chainsaw on the ground, he primed it and pinned it down with one hand and a knee and yanked the pull cord with the other. It sputtered, showing signs of wanting to start. He pulled again and again and the engine screamed and the chain whipped around the blade. Blue smoke kicked out of the exhaust and Bill let it idle. It ran rough so he adjusted the throttle. Once he was convinced it was in full working order, he shut it off and took it with him into the house.

"I'm going to cut that damn tree down if it kills me. I'll let the police finish up whatever they're doing, and then I'll get to work without anyone interfering," Bill said. This madness needed to stop, and this was the only remedy he could think of. Jim was right, in a sense.

He set the saw down next to the front door, not caring about the grime it shed onto the floor.

"You need to know that Jim is no longer alive," Bill said into the house. He spoke loudly. "I think you should move on now. There's nothing left for you to stick around for. The police are going to rescue Bridget. She's that kidnapped girl I was telling you about. The tree will be gone soon. I'm going to cut it down, cutting off every limb right down to the trunk where I'll turn it into a stump. So why don't you go on now and be at peace?"

Bill entered the kitchen and saw that all the cabinet doors were open, the dishes were smashed on the floor, and the chairs at the table were tipped over. He couldn't believe his eyes.

TRAVIS KIDWELL AND WEST PALM BEACH OFFICERS

Officer Frank Marshall arrived at the house with his partner, Officer Medina Armana. Both officers had over ten years of experience on the Palm Beach Police Force, and never had they heard of anything as bizarre as this Devil Tree nonsense coming out of Port Saint Lucie. The Treasure Coast sounded more like the Trash Coast.

When they first got the call from the Port Saint Lucie Police Department requesting their assistance, they were asked to check in on a woman named Elizabeth Brown. Both Officers Marshall and Armana knew of the woman and how she was involved in the case, so the briefing went quick. She was one of the two girls who had escaped Schaeffer's evil, and they were responsible for his reign of terror coming to an end.

Marshall and Armana were asked to follow up on the license plate of a person who had picked up Ms. Brown earlier in the day.

According to records, this young man had no direct relation to Elizabeth Brown.

Officer Frank Marshall reviewed his notes, which reminded him that the name of the person in question was Travis Kidwell. They had just pulled up to his last known address.

"They have some freaky shit going on up there in Saint Lucie County," Marshall said.

"A haunted tree, a cult, and now the only two people who were able to escape Schaeffer have possibly been abducted—yeah, that would definitely qualify as freaky shit in my book," Armana said.

Officer Marshall radioed dispatch. "Arrived on site."

"Ten-four," dispatch responded.

Armana took out her flashlight and tapped the heavy wooden door to the otherwise typical Florida home: stucco, with a paver driveway and tall palm trees.

They waited a few minutes, and Marshall looked around the sides of the house. Saint Augustine grass crunched underfoot and took away any element of surprise if someone were hiding there.

"The house looks dark, and I don't think the vehicle is here," Armana said.

Locks on the door slid audibly, and Officer Armana faced the door. "Or not," she said and her hand hovered near her weapon. Her partner took his weapon out of the holster and kept it at his side. The angle he stood at was optimum in case things turned ugly.

"Yes?" a little old lady said. Her hair was gray and messy. She wore a nightgown that had a floral design similar to the one Schaeffer had worn.

"Palm Beach Police, ma'am. I'm Officer Medina Armana, and my partner over there is Officer Frank Marshall."

Without warning, the woman backed away quickly and slammed the door shut and locked it. Armana looked at Marshall, the two equally confused. Armana tapped her flashlight on the door again, this time with a bit more force.

"Can you please open the door so we can ask you a few questions?" she said.

"How do I know you're the real police?" the woman said, her voice muffled and afraid.

"We are the real police," Armana said and shook her head at her partner.

"I'm sure if you weren't the police you'd tell me that too."

"Go ahead and call 911 and they will verify that we are indeed the real police. We want you to feel safe."

Frank Marshall radioed dispatch. "The resident inside won't open the door until she knows we are the real police."

"Ten-four," dispatch said, and an electronic bleep squawked through both officers' radios.

Officer Marshall holstered his weapon, and they waited. About a minute later, the lady opened the door and shuffled forward. "I'm sorry," she said. "You can never be too careful nowadays; especially with all the strange things going on in this world."

"I absolutely agree with you Mrs. —?" Armana said.

"McGary. But don't you know that before you come here?"

"Yes. I'm just checking to make sure I have the right person."

"What do you want with me? I'm just an old woman."

"I just want to ask you a few questions if that is OK."

She nodded, and the flab underneath her chin wiggled. "OK, I can answer them, I think."

"I appreciate that."

"Before you get started, I wanted to say that sometimes I hear about people impersonating the police officers, and they force their way into the house," Mrs. McGary said. "I forget what they call it."

"That would be a home invasion," Officer Armana said.

"That's it," Mrs. McGary said. She tried to snap her fingers, but they were gnarled from time. "I guess what I'm saying is please don't be upset with me. I'm just trying to protect myself."

"I'm not upset with you at all, Mrs. McGary. Like I said, I'd just like to ask you a few simple questions, and then I'll get out of your hair."

She patted her head. "Speaking of which, I don't think I brushed my hair today. Maybe I should go inside and make myself look a little more presentable. Don't you think?"

"No, Mrs. McGary, that won't be necessary, really."

"That doesn't make me feel comfortable."

"I won't look, and I won't judge. I promise."

She looked at the officer with eyes that had seen many changes, both good and bad, throughout her long life. "I don't want to be a victim ever again."

"I'm sorry, Mrs. McGary?"

"That's why I was so cautious."

"Can you tell me what you were a victim of?"

The old lady shook her head and looked away. "I don't want to talk about that right now. I'd rather forget it. My life is getting shorter by the minute, so why don't you ask me the questions you were talking about?"

Officer Armana shifted from one foot to the other. "Does Travis Kidwell live here with you, ma'am?"

"No," she replied, looking away from Officer Armana.

"Mrs. McGary, I need you to be as forthcoming with me as possible. This is a very serious thing we are investigating, and a young woman's life is at stake here."

The old woman grumbled something under her breath and rolled her lips underneath her toothless gums. "Well, no, he doesn't live here. Not anymore."

Officer Marshall walked around the rear of the house. Having been through this so many times, the procedure was like clockwork.

"Do you know an Elizabeth Brown or have you ever heard of her?" Armana asked.

She thought for a long moment. "No, I can't say that I have. Why, is she the girl who's in trouble?"

"I believe so. Do you mind if I come inside and look around?"

"No, not at all," the old lady said and backed into the house.

Armana clicked her radio. A quick double click answered. She entered the home and began to look around.

"Who is Travis Kidwell to you?"

"He was a renter but more like a squatter. He finally left here about four months ago."

"Did he say where he was going?"

"No."

"How about maybe saying something in passing that you might've overheard?"

She chewed her lips. "No. Even if he did, I probably wouldn't have thought it important and would have forgotten about it. My memory isn't all that good either."

"You're doing just fine."

Mrs. McGary stood up straight and made a face of pain while she did so. "I'm glad he left, even though he owed me about six month's worth of rent."

Armana took some notes. "Anything you can tell me about Travis that might help me find where he is?"

"No," Mrs. McGary said and shook her head. "Just that he was weird and hung out with weird people."

"Can you define that for me?"

She shrugged.

"Why did you get that impression from him?"

"He dressed in dark clothing all the time. He wore odd jewelry and painted his fingernails black."

"Did you see what kind of jewelry?"

She nodded her head. "Yes. Things that shouldn't be in a Christian household, that's for sure." She shrank into herself again. "I saw upside down stars in his room, candle circles, and some other things I can't and don't care to remember. Something to do with a goat man or something . . . I don't know. I may be old, but I'm not stupid. I knew what he was doing, and I despised him doing that in my house and I told him so. I also told him if he wasn't going to pay rent he would have to go. That's when he got upset the most. He always had an excuse. Before the anger would come he would tell me he lost his job, had other bills to pay, was broke and would pay me soon." She shook her head. "I mean what about me? I live off of Social Security."

Armana nodded. "I'm sorry about your troubles with him. You should have called us."

"I was afraid to." Her body shook. "I remember this one time I walked into his room and I found him sitting in the center of these lit candles. He was wearing a black robe and had this really frightening red mask on. As soon as he looked at me, he rushed me and got me out of the room. I could barely stand the way he was handling me. He told me the best thing I could do was to mind my own business." Her eyes were bright with tears. "So that's what I did. I didn't want any trouble, so I just kept to myself. I was better off. I knew if I prayed long and hard enough, the Good Lord would get him away from me."

"I understand," Armana said and clicked her radio twice, and a single click answered. "I thank you for allowing me inside and talking to me. If you happen to run into Travis, please don't tell him we're looking for him. It might just make him mad." She handed the old woman a business card. "Just give me a call and let me handle him. I promise you no harm will come to you."

"OK."

Armana exited the home and met up with her partner. "Anything?"

Officer Marshall shook his head. "Everything is as normal as this day is hot." He tugged on the weight of his vest. "What did you get?"

"That this Travis Kidwell guy is an odd duck and a squatter. From what Mrs. McGary was telling me, I have the impression that this guy might be involved with the cult."

"What was she telling you?"

"She said he wore strange jewelry, something about a goat man, and also described the jewelry as not belonging inside a Christian house. Upside down stars, black painted fingernails, and a black robe and red mask. She was scared of him."

"Not good," Marshall said and looked away. He turned his chin up to the sun. "You going to call what's-his-name over there in Saint Lucie and let him know?"

"I'll do it unless you want to do it."

Marshall lowered his chin and shook his head. "It's a mess, and now this thing is starting to spill into Palm Beach, too. I don't like it, and I would like to get these guys before what they're doing becomes a scourge. That's the last thing we need."

"I got it," Armana said and pulled out her phone and dialed.

"Abernathy," the man on the other end said.

"It's Armana from the Palm Beach Police Department."

"Thank you for your promptness. What did you guys come up with?"

"Nothing good," Armana said. "It seems this Travis Kidwell is quite possibly affiliated with the cult over there. The address tied to his plates is outdated. He moved on and gave the old woman he was renting from quite the scare. The description she gave us almost places him at that tree."

"And let me guess." Abernathy breathed through the phone. "She doesn't know where he went."

"That's right . . . and even if she did know, I doubt she'd tell us anyway. She's understandably afraid of this guy. We've got our ears up, and if we come up with anything, we'll let you know."

There was a long beat of silence.

"Damn," Abernathy said. "It sounds like they have both girls now." Armana could hear him hit something. "I don't know why that girl didn't go with my officer when our captain sent him there to offer her protection."

"You can lead a horse to water . . . "

"Hey, thank you for looking into this for us. We appreciate it."

"You're welcome. And good luck."

Chapter 34

CHECKING THE TREE

Officer Ezekiel Frey drove the police cruiser into Oak Hammock Park and allowed the vehicle to coast through the empty parking lot.

Night had fallen, and the tension between Frey and his partner, Gideon Wallingford, kept the two men quiet and serious. What they were told to do by their captain in a place where one of their own was tortured and killed made this grave in every way. Normally, they spoke about everything from their home lives and hobbies to their college days and girlfriends from the past. But not this night, and certainly not here. There were killers in the brush waiting for more victims, and neither one of them was willing to go without a fight if they were confronted.

"Not us," Officer Frey said.

"What's that?" Wallingford said, his eyes wide as he searched the area.

"Not us. Not tonight," Frey responded in a tone that was both nervous and focused.

Officer Wallingford sat in the passenger seat and shined the spotlight into the surrounding trees, nearby canal, and playground and then shut it off.

"All clear," Wallingford said.

"That's a good start," Frey said and stopped the vehicle next to the C-24 canal fence and shut off the engine. The two officers looked at one another; each gave a nod and exited the vehicle. They lit their flashlights and drew their weapons.

Although it was about a quarter mile walk from the fence to the path that led to the Devil Tree, they weren't taking any chances. Their orders were clear: sweep the parking lot, get out of the cruiser, and check the area surrounding the tree. Don't make any effort to discover anyone, but make sure you protect yourselves first. Make it seem like we don't know the women have been taken. Routine walks.

Their flashlight beams worked the path, the tree line, and the steep slope that dropped into the canal. The aim of their pistols followed the roving swing of their lights, and nervous fingers curled around the triggers.

"I feel like we're walking into an ambush," Officer Frey said.

"Keep it down," Officer Wallingford whispered back. "Stay on point as planned, and let's watch each other's backs. We stick together and keep a clear head. We do that, we're going to be fine."

Frey nodded and then shivered. He looked at Wallingford and knew he could trust him with his life. He seemed on task and alert. Frey noted that some people felt the tree and others did not; from the appearance of it, the tree had no supernatural effect on Wallingford.

The two officers turned onto the path that subtly hooked right, and their flashlight beams soon found the Devil Tree. The ancient goliath stretched across the forest, the canopy taking over the other trees; the massive scarred trunk stood as a reminder of the bad things that happened there. The gape in the side of the tree where the cement patch once covered the occult engravings looked like an entryway to Hell. Frey silently hoped that it wasn't a sentinel, watching and waiting for bad things yet to come.

Their shafts of light brushed over the surrounding forest, and eerie shadows the foliage cast played tricks on their minds. Both officers maintained their calm and acted like they were searching the area and looking for anyone who might have hidden if they had heard the officers' approach.

"All is quiet," Wallingford said and holstered his weapon.

Frey concentrated his beam on his partner and holstered his weapon, too. "Yeah. I think things will be quiet since they picked up that Dalton Vyle kid. The captain is adamant that we caught the right one."

"Caught or not, this place gives me the creeps. Guys like that should be locked up for a long time."

"I agree. With everything that has gone on here, how could he not be put away for the rest of his life?"

Officer Wallingford centered his light on the path that would lead them back toward the C-24 fence and ultimately their squad car.

"Come on, let's get out of here," Wallingford said. "I doubt anyone is stupid enough to come here tonight. If there was anyone else involved in this, they'd have to know we'd be all over the place, and in force, looking to get them to avenge Lenza's death."

"No one said criminals are smart. But I can tell you I won't miss this place."

"Me neither. Should we skip the next visit?"

"Sounds like a good idea to me. There's no one else. They got him."

The two men relaxed as they exited the Devil Tree path and walked back to their squad car. Before Ezekiel Frey entered the patrol car, he clicked his radio and simply said, "All clear."

They got into their cruiser and left Oak Hammock Park, breathing a little easier on their way out, hoping what they did was enough to bring Abernathy's plan to life.

Chapter 32

CAMO

Briston Nowar had been lying beneath leaves, sticks, and natural debris scattered on the forest floor near the Devil Tree. He had volunteered to see if the police were going to come to the tree this night and to find out what they knew about Bridget and Elizabeth.

He had watched two officers walk around the tree and search the immediate area. They had even shined their flashlight on him two or three times, but his dark clothing and camouflage face paint aided in his concealment.

The conversation between the two officers had proven to be interesting, and all of his time waiting there, remaining still, peeing in his pants and ignoring every itch so as not to give himself away was worth it.

He had served the cause, and when he returned to report what he had learned, indeed would he be elevated in the group and shown appreciation by all the members.

Fifteen minutes or more had passed since the officers left the area, and he slowly rose. Brushing the debris from his clothing, he navigated the forest with stealth. Once he neared the perimeter, he shed his clothes and donned new ones, removed his face paint, and walked the streets, casual in his travel so he didn't draw any unnecessary attention to himself if a patrol unit were to pass him by.

Briston, dressed now in his black robe and concealed by the red mask, entered a large room lit by candles. The brick walls and dirt floor echoed with his every step. The abandoned building was a perfect place for the congregation to meet.

He approached the gathered leaders of the cult and remained silent until he was addressed.

"What's the news, brother?" One in a robe and white mask said.

"Two officers showed up at the tree, and I could hear their every word."

"So the location we chose for you to hide in was a good one?"

"It was perfect." He wished they could see his smile. "While they were having a look around and talking to each other, they revealed that the captain of police believes Dalton acted alone. I believe he held up under their questioning."

The gathered members muttered their praise for Dalton's faithfulness to the assembly.

"I listened carefully, and they didn't mention a thing about Bridget or Elizabeth," Briston said.

"This is great news," another dressed in a black robe said, his face concealed by the white mask; the flicker of candlelight made the plastic expression appear twisted and grotesque. "They must not know of their disappearance. This will allow us to move ahead with our plans tomorrow. We will act when they think we won't."

"We will give the tree the sacrifices it has been longing for."

"Tomorrow can't come soon enough," Briston said.

"It will be here before you know it. Take pride in knowing you have served the cause as well, as Dalton did. Reveal your work to no one."

"I won't," Briston bowed. "Thank you for trusting in me."

"Go now, for we must make plans so that everything is perfect for tomorrow. We need to send a message to the people of this community. Kill who should be killed and sacrifice them upon the tree."

"As you wish." Briston bowed again and left the gathering feeling proud about what he had done and excited for what was to come.

Chapter ③③

THE HOLE

Bridget couldn't stop shaking. The deep cold that seeped from the moist soil had sopped her clothing and covered her skin in a chilled embrace. Her teeth chattered, and it wreaked havoc with the pain it caused her dislocated jaw. The pain, her will, and her hands couldn't stop them from slamming together.

The darkness had now fallen for the second time since her incarceration, and it made it impossible to see an inch in front of her face. Stomach pains from hunger made her shake, and she pushed a fist into her stomach to help chase away the ache. Her muscles cramped and forced her flat on the ground.

Sleep had come and gone as she battled her ailments and watched the hatch with a waning interest. She was unsure how long she had been in this hole but knew it was at least two nights now. She was convinced she was left to starve to death. It had been awhile since she had seen anyone, and she couldn't remember the last time she heard anyone or anything. Not the sound of a bird or the pattering of feet from an animal.

She was so weak she was sure she couldn't move and didn't try. It didn't matter because she was in a box with high dirt walls, a dirt floor, and the way out dangling over her head, teasing her.

She'd spent hours going over the moment she had been attacked. What if she had done things differently? Would she have stood a fighting chance against her attackers if she used more caution to open the door? There was no doubt she would have, but she thought for sure it was the police who had come to get her and protect her. This was the second time they let her down. Before she had even realized what was happening to her, she was flat on her back and stars were filling her head from hitting the hard floor and the immediate assault of heavy punches from thick fists that crashed into her face.

Why didn't she look through the peephole before she opened the door? The thought haunted her and angered her.

"Stupid," she said, the word a mumble.

The grimy layer of filth that stuck to her also seemed to intensify the chill that bit her flesh. The pain in her face had mostly gone away, but the swelling still held her eye shut and puffed her cheek. Her jaw was a completely different story.

Her thoughts shifted to Dalton and how he had fooled her. To think she had a long lost friend looking to rekindle a friendship that had gone cold so long ago—it had turned out to be a horrible lie. Why wasn't she able to piece together the time line? He started coming around once the incident with Schaeffer was broadcast across the news. A visit here and there at first, and then he began to show up more frequently, asking her how she was, claiming to be checking up on her.

"I am a fool," she said, and for one bewildering moment she thought she heard a response. She dismissed it, returning to the thought of this and so many other things playing in her head and toying with her emotions.

Sounds from above drew her attention and quieted her mind. There were voices and the crunch of sticks underfoot. She hoped to hear the whine of a dog. That would be a telltale sign that it was law enforcement conducting a search and finally finding her.

The slab that covered the hole slid away, and the people moving it struggled. She could see it because whoever was above held onto a flashlight or lantern, and the pale light surrounded them and filled the hole.

"Hello?" she said optimistically, hoping with everything she had that what appeared to be black robes was just a trick of the light or a figment of a mind deprived of nourishment.

A ladder made of two long tree branches and thick sticks tied in place by vine cordage making up the rungs slid into the hole and stuck out of the top, giving her the chance to climb out if she could muster the strength. When she pushed herself to her feet, her legs shook and her breath was gone in an instant, as was her balance. She held onto the wall.

Using her hands to help guide her along, step by step, she approached the ladder and ignored her partial numbness and the pain that made up everything else.

"Thank you," she said and felt her lips cracking and bleeding.

"I wouldn't do anything stupid," a voice called down to her, and she looked up. Multiple masked faces stared down at her; their black robes were no trick of light, and neither were the creepy dark masks that contorted in the lamplight.

"No," she said and fell to her knees. "Please."

"Stand and come up on your own or we will come down and get you," a muffled voice said. "If we come down, you're going to feel worse than you do right now."

Bridget looked up. She didn't feel like going and didn't know if she could even if she wanted to. In a sense, she didn't care what they did to her. As morbid as it sounded, she preferred that they kill her in this hole rather than at the tree. At least that would give her soul a chance to escape the evil that bound things there.

"Have you ever been stabbed, Bridget?"

She looked up and whimpered.

A knife was being twirled in the light, and the blade gleamed.

"This sinks into the skin like it's butter. If you don't believe me, remain on your knees. Make me come down there and get you."

The threat was effective enough to get her to change her mind and stand. Without hope there was nothing to cling to, so she pushed on. She walked to the ladder and placed a foot on the first rung and rested her head for a second. She looked up, and the hole looked like a vortex. It made her feel dizzy and she worried she might pass out.

"Climb up," the voice from above said. This time someone else was talking to her.

"I'm coming," she said with a voice driven by the desire to survive but imbued with a weakness so profound that only her will moved her along. She struggled with each step, and as she neared the top, she could feel a nighttime breeze that smelled fresh and played with the chill that clung to her. She realized in that moment: Life was beautiful, and she wasn't ready to die. Not for this cause and not like this.

"Don't do anything stupid. There are many of us, and you are alone and are so weak you can barely stand."

"I won't," she said.

"I know that. Because you can't," another said. "You are as helpless as a newborn."

"We starved you because we know what you're capable of. We know everything about you, and you're going to pay for what you did to Schaeffer and what you deprived the tree of."

There were no words to defend herself against such outlandish allegations. These people were maniacs in every sense of the word. How could so many people believe in what Schaeffer did? Why would they want to continue acting out in his name?

When she finally made it out of the hole, she had no answers to the many questions she asked herself, and so she just flopped onto the ground. The smell of leaves filled her senses; it was so much more pleasant than the dirt.

"To your feet," an angry voice said.

Yanked to her feet, they shook her, and her arms flailed and her knees buckled. The lamplight revealed that she had been in some sort of ancient ruin. Broken cinderblock walls were all over the place. The frame of what appeared to have been a house or some sort of small building was what concealed the secret basement.

The masked group dragged her through the forest, and she was so fatigued she couldn't get her feet underneath her. Her feet left two tracks in the forest floor—that would be the last thing she left behind on this earth, she thought. But with that, she took comfort in knowing her pain would end. She would leave the beauty of life behind.

"We're taking you to the tree," someone taunted. "When you get there, you are going to have to answer for what you have done. And just so you know, there isn't a single answer that will save you. We just want to hear you beg."

Chapter 34

LISTEN TO THE SILENCE

Candlelight surrounded the tree, and Bridget whimpered at the ceremony of it all. Helpless to stop what was about to happen to her, she could only watch the people around her perform their rituals.

A dozen or more people dressed in black robes and plastic masks had surrounded the tree. They broke their circle to allow her passage, indicating that they had been waiting for her.

Dragged close to the tree, she was dropped on the ground. She hit her head on a thick root that bulged above the surface of dirt, re-injuring the same part of her skull that had been slammed to the floor inside her home when they took her.

She groaned and watched the circle close around her. People of all different sizes were looking down on her, and she knew something awful was going to happen. Suffering and torment was something she was sure of.

A member stepped forward and bound her wrists behind her back and then forced her into the kneeling position. Another member stepped forward, guided her chin to get her attention, and removed a long curved knife and waved it around menacingly. The masked figure touched her face with the tip and drew blood. The cold helped numb her sliced flesh but not enough to keep her from wincing and pulling away.

"You must know this is what the tree wanted," someone said. "Although you foiled Schaeffer's plan to give you to the tree, to provide it with the nourishment it needs, we are here to finish what he started. There's something about you that it needs. And as your body breaks down around its ancient trunk and is absorbed through its intricate rooting system, its required taste shall be satisfied, and you will have the honor of living on forever through its branches and leaves, protected by its thick, impenetrable bark."

Bridget began to weep, but tears couldn't roll down her dry face.

"You are going to be another blood sacrifice to Baphomet. This is his throne, and we hope he will approve."

Another cloaked person squatted in front of Bridget, masked face at her eye level. Reaching up with the hand that didn't hold the knife, the figure pulled the mask off and then rolled the hood back. Bridget gasped and fell back. With a newfound burst of energy, she kicked her feet and pushed herself against the tree and shook her head.

"No, no, no!" she said, the pain in her jaw forgotten.

"What's wrong?" Elizabeth said with a smile.

"I don't understand," Bridget said, her words slurred.

"How don't you understand?" Elizabeth said. "You couldn't feel the pull? You couldn't hear it calling out to you?"

"No," Bridget said, and her friend's face collapsed into sadness.

"That is why you're in the position you're in." Elizabeth got up and circled the tree. She ran her hand across the trunk as she looked up into the massive canopy. "You just need to embrace the silence and listen to what it has to say to you."

"What happened to you, Elizabeth?"

"I listened, Bridget." She stopped circling and walked over to Bridget, knelt, and took her hand. "That's why I had you placed in that hole. I wanted to give you a chance to hear the tree. To understand that it wants us."

"What are you talking about? The tree doesn't want us. It is just a tree."

"Blasphemy," Elizabeth shouted and slapped Bridget, and sparks of pain exploded in her head. "You didn't listen to the voice in your head while I had you in solitary, and you're not listening now."

Bridget turned away, expecting another slap, but it never came. "Did you organize this?"

"I had instruction," Elizabeth said. "I couldn't stop thinking about the tree and hearing it call out to me. When I came here by myself, it would ask me about you. That's why I brought you to the tree. I wanted it to see you and to understand what it wanted with you. Now I know."

"What are you talking about, Elizabeth? We were best friends! We survived an attack from one of the worst serial killers Florida has ever seen!"

"We were," Elizabeth said. "It's funny how things change. The influences that guide us and the people who are willing to come along . . . I see you are not one of them, and that's why I know what the tree wants from you."

Elizabeth put on her white mask and raised her hood. She tilted her face down toward Bridget, her head turned ever so slightly as if she were inspecting her, trying to figure out how her mind worked.

"It wants her blood," Elizabeth said, her voice sounding totally different with the mask on. "It wants everything that's inside of her, everything that believes it is pure but is really tainted. Kill her. I want to hear her scream!"

THE SILENCE BROKEN

Lights on the outskirts of the trees shined on everyone, and the shouts of many men and women broke their cover as they stepped out of the tree line with their weapons drawn. They closed in on the cult with enough speed to both cause mayhem and control the outcome.

The tactic was called shock and awe.

"Police! Put your fucking hands where I can see them!" an officer shouted.

"Don't you move a muscle or I'll blow your brains out," another officer shouted.

"Keep your hands where I can see them!"

All the orders came at once, and the barks from German Shepherds that were eager to take down the bad guys only added to the chaos.

"Everyone get down on the ground, and don't move," an officer said above all the rest.

"No! Not when we are so close," Elizabeth screamed. "Don't give yourself up. Sacrifice them or yourself! Don't you let them take you out of this forest alive. If you die here, you give the tree what it needs!"

The people in black robes began to run at the police and they were tased and fell like dominoes. Elizabeth raised the knife over her head and her mask clattered to the forest floor. A look of someone possessed took over her face as she motioned to bring the knife down into Bridget's chest. "I will have my sacrifice!"

Pow. Pow.

Officer Abernathy hit Elizabeth once in the shoulder and a second time in the back of the neck. She dropped the knife, dropped to her knees, gurgled on blood that filled her mouth, and twisted and slumped forward, dead. Draped across Bridget's lap, her body twitched, and her eyes remained open.

"Oh, Elizabeth," Bridget said, making no attempt to get out from underneath her friend. She looked into her open eyes and wondered how someone so good, so innocent and docile, could be turned into this. Bridget looked up into the canopy of the tree and thought she saw something scamper higher up into the overhead foliage. "It didn't have to come to this."

All around, the police outnumbered the cult three to one and took them down without having to kill anyone else.

Abernathy walked over to Bridget and pulled Elizabeth off of her. He took a knee. "Paramedics are already on their way into the forest," he said. "Don't move, and let them look you over."

Bridget reached out and hugged Abernathy. Her chest heaved as she tried to absorb everything that just happened.

"I know," Abernathy said. "I'm just as surprised as you. I thought for sure Travis Kidwell was the leader and kidnapped Elizabeth. I thought they were going to bring Elizabeth here with you and use you both as a sacrifice. I'm so sorry. I had no idea she was a part of this."

Bridget squeezed harder, her newfound strength driven by pure emotion.

"Abernathy," Breck said and pulled on Abernathy's shoulder. "Travis Kidwell isn't even here."

Abernathy gently broke away from Bridget's hold. She leaned against the tree and cried. Her lap was covered with her friend's blood and her lifeless body lay only a few feet away.

"Say that again," Abernathy said.

"Travis Kidwell—he's not here."

Abernathy stood and looked at all the unmasked cult members. "I need to borrow someone's keys."

A nearby officer tossed Abernathy his keys. "1201, parked near the entrance of the park," the officer told Abernathy.

"Officer Breck is going to take care of you," he said to Bridget. Abernathy ran away, driven by pure desperation.

"Where are you going?" Breck called after him, but Abernathy didn't reply.

Chapter ③⑥

A GHOST

Bill found himself pacing the floor in his bedroom. His thoughts were consumed by what he knew was unfolding at the park. He wished he could be there so he knew for sure that everything had turned out all right. He hoped that planting false information on his blog had made the cult act as Abernathy had predicted. That would make him a part of something great.

Each minute that passed felt like an hour, and his palms were drenched with sweat and his legs carried him around in circles he was only vaguely aware he was walking.

Abernathy said he would call as soon as he could and would let him know what happened. But not knowing what was going on and when he might get that phone call made Bill restless, worried, and frustrated.

A sound of someone rummaging around the other side of the mobile home interrupted his thoughts, and he paused to listen.

It seemed to be the first time he heard Susan since he told her about Jim and his suicide. He thought she had moved on like he suggested, but maybe she liked being in the house.

He sat on the edge of the bed and waited for the sounds to stop. But they continued. Quiet and curious, it sounded like she was rummaging through the cabinets. Then he remembered how she had opened them and tipped the chair over. Was she still upset over the news he had told her?

He walked toward the living room and stopped there for a moment to listen to the sounds that didn't stop.

"Odd," Bill said to himself and went into the kitchen. The sight of seeing someone standing inside his house struck him with fear so deep he didn't move and didn't utter a single word. He just looked at the person who stood there looking back at him. A black robe covered the figure's body and a hood was pulled over the head. A white mask with eye holes and no mouth disturbed him. The plastic mold was shaped into something wicked and awful.

"You've become quite the nuisance," the person behind the mask said and untied his silk belt with tassels at the ends. Although his voice was muffled, his words were clear. "You will not be given the chance to impede on our missions any longer and attempt to thwart our movement. For we are Legion, and we are many."

Bill turned to run away, but his attacker was upon him before he took his second step. He leapt onto his back and dragged him to the ground. The cloaked intruder wrapped the silk belt around Bill's neck and pulled it tight. The pressure in Bill's face made his eyes bulge, and a strange feeling filled his head. A living wall of blackness started to come over him.

"No," the guy behind the mask said and let go of the belt. Slowly, the black receded and Bill coughed. He was rolled over to his back.

The man descended upon him, straddling his chest. "I want you to feel it!"

The intruder brandished a knife and raised it above his head and plunged it deep into Bill's chest over and over again. Bill's body stiffened with pain, each blow taking away his feeling. His mouth filled with blood, and he watched the knife move up and down, slinging his blood all over the room as it cleaved through his chest. He reached up to try to remove the mask so he could look his killer in the eyes, but he had lost too much sensation, and the darkness closed in around him.

Travis Kidwell removed his hood and mask, panting with the surge of adrenaline that was satisfied by the warmth of his victim's blood.

Knowing he had little time before they figured it out, he used Bill's blood to write on the wall.

This is just the beginning.

He ran out the door and into the cover of night, knowing this was far from over. There was work to be done.

Chapter ③④

THE LEGEND LIVES

Abernathy slammed his fist into the steering wheel as he raced toward Bill Faulkner's house. How didn't he see this play coming? Had his time with Schaeffer affected him so that he lost his uncanny ability to notice the obscure details in situations and conditions?

To protect and serve was the oath he'd taken, and he took it very seriously.

He stepped on the gas pedal, and a sense of dread made him grit his teeth. Taking a corner too tight, his rear wheels hit the curb and the cruiser bounced.

"I better be wrong," he shouted but knew he wasn't. It was their play, and now that he saw it too late, it was going to cost someone else their life.

This was their way to keep this ugly thing alive. To make him and others around him pay. It was something more than a tree where a deranged man killed his unfortunate victims. It had become a beacon where the unholy gathered and attempted to steal the souls of innocents and offer them up to something so wicked and unbelievable that Abernathy found even his own soul darkening.

Hitting one last turn, he arrived at Bill's house. The memories of getting pounded in the back of the head by Jim flooded though his mind, and caution wanted to slow him down, but he didn't listen to it. Jim was just another innocent changed by his interaction with the tree and the surrounding area.

"I will resist," he said as he jumped out of the cruiser and charged up the walkway. Slamming into the door with his shoulder, the weakened doorjamb broke away and Abernathy stopped cold and read the message scrawled on the wall with blood. He readied himself to look down at Bill's lifeless body.

A pool of blood soaked the carpet and surrounded the blogger's body. His chest had a gaping hole in it, and some of his innards hung out the same way as when they had disemboweled Officer Lenza. There was some sort of rope around Bill's neck. He had suffered badly.

Abernathy turned away a changed man. Two men had experienced horrific deaths at the hands of a new serial killer. A killer who had a motive that was controlled by his own ex-partner, now dead and buried, and a tree that people perceived to be possessed.

"I've had enough," Abernathy said. He turned and noticed the chainsaw and gas. Bill was going to try to cut down the tree. Maybe that's what needed to be done. Maybe it was what should have been done six months ago. They should have tried harder.

Abernathy stepped outside with a slam of the door, and he pressed the button on his radio. "I have a twenty-one, thirty-four, five at 2550 Oak Lane."

"Ten-four," dispatch responded. "I'm sending a ten-seventy-one."

Abernathy sat on the stoop, the thought of taking that chainsaw to that tree burning through his veins. Someone needed to do something, including burning down this house. Things would just keep repeating themselves over and over, and he saw no end in sight.

At the very least he would lobby to the county commissioners for the tree and home where two homicides were committed to be removed. It was the only way to stop the madness. If they didn't see it his way, he would do it himself.

Chapter 38

SELF-DOUBT

Officer Abernathy waited until the ambulance came before he ceased standing guard over Bill's body. That was the least he could do for the man he'd used to try to stop a killer cult. Guilt was something heavy and crushing, and Abernathy didn't know if he could bear the weight.

Driving back to Oak Hammock Park, when he pulled into the parking lot, he saw Bridget strapped to a stretcher that was being loaded into an ambulance. She looked like hell.

Abernathy exited the vehicle, handed off the keys, and walked past the C-24 canal sign to the Devil Tree. All of the cult members had been removed from the area and taken to the closest jail. Elizabeth's body was covered with a white sheet, and his bullet casings had been found and flagged by forensics, who crawled all over the place like ants pouring out of a mound.

Breck was talking to the captain when they both noticed Abernathy.

"Job well done," the captain said.

Abernathy felt something in his chest swell and threaten to bust out. He shook his head and pushed down what he felt. What happened tonight was not a job well done.

"You're going to need to talk to forensics," the captain said. "I'm sorry to hear about the reporter guy."

"Bill Faulkner," Abernathy said. The debt he felt was so deep he could never pay him back; he felt he'd never be able to do enough to honor Bill's memory. "I think he needs to be recognized by the department for his assistance in helping us solve this case."

"I agree," the captain said and clapped Abernathy's shoulder. "I know you don't think so, but it was a good job. You can't be everywhere at the same time."

Abernathy looked at his feet, and the captain walked away.

"Pick your head up and follow me," Breck said.

Breck walked through the thick brush and spoke as he made his own path. "I spoke to Bridget while the paramedics were attending to her," he said as they came upon the foundations to the buildings that once stood in the remote part of the forest. "She said this was where they kept her after they abducted her from the house."

Abernathy looked and didn't see what Breck was talking about. Collapsed walls, dirt, leaves, large round rocks, and flat rocks littered the ground.

Breck walked over to the slate in the middle of one of the foundations.

"Come over here and give me a hand," Breck said.

He stood opposite Breck, and they took hold of the slab and slid it away. A gaping hole in the ground opened up.

Anger turned Abernathy away. He had been standing right there just days before and didn't see what he was being shown. He had looked hard, feeling something was there, but he'd given up because he believed he was looking at nothing.

"She was deprived of light and food in this old cellar, which served as her prison."

Abernathy looked into the hole and saw a handmade ladder at the bottom. He couldn't imagine. His head swam, and he needed to sit.

There was no doubt about it. He'd lost his touch, and it cost someone their life and someone else emotional distress that would probably disable her from ever having any sense of normalcy in her life. Also, there was a killer at large, and he had nowhere to begin to search for him. It was like his soul just fell into that hole, never to come out again.

His hand went to his badge pinned to his shirt. A part of him wanted to rip it off and toss it so deep into the forest they could never find it. He should walk away from all of this and let someone who hadn't been so deeply affected by everything take a crack at it. His sidearm would look lovely in his mouth.

"I know what you're thinking," Breck said. "I don't even need to ask because I see it on your face and your clenched fists. Let it go."

Abernathy looked down, not having realized that his fists were balled. He relaxed his hands; he didn't want Breck pointing things out to him when he was the one who always used to do that.

"I showed you this because you needed to know," Breck said. "Your intuition is there. You just need to trust yourself. You thought there was something here, but you didn't say anything to me when you should have. I know Schaeffer took that away from you the day you discovered his deceit. It is up to you to get it back. Don't quit on us and the people who need you. Oh, and forensics found pictures of the ruins on Lenza's phone. He forwarded them to his wife but didn't say anything to anyone either."

Breck walked away, and Abernathy stared at the hole. His friend's words were perfect, but it was like they bounced off of him and fell into that pit, joining the part of him that cared. He felt so alone, and self-doubt consumed him so much that all he could do was clamp his eyes shut and try to fight away the tears.

But this right here—what he felt—was something he would never get over. To try to imagine the horror Bill suffered because he'd asked him to help by posting phony reports—Abernathy couldn't bring himself to do it. And to know that a young woman was tossed into this hole with no way out—that was exactly how he felt.

Maybe he needed to hand in his badge and gun before he did something stupid. Maybe the word 'maybe' needed to be removed from his thinking process and he should just do what he knew needed to be done.

Chapter ③⑨

THE DEVIL'S SEED

It had been two months since the incidents at the tree played out. A police officer he knew as Abernathy was continuing to lobby that the Devil Tree be removed, and his activities were being closely followed by the media.

Travis Kidwell took a great interest in what Officer Abernathy was doing and was concerned that he might be successful. People in the town were behind him, though the young people remained curious about the haunted tree and woods that surrounded it.

Dressed in khaki shorts, deck shoes with no socks, and a polo shirt with the collar popped, he peered out from behind mirrored sunglasses. His hair was neatly parted to the side, and the sweater tossed over his shoulders and tied around his neck made him look like a college kid who was here visiting relatives and just out for a stroll.

Eating a bag of chips and taking his time, he casually walked past the C-24 canal sign and followed the narrow dirt path that some Saint Augustine grass had grown over. Looking into the canal, he took his time and watched the running water, searched for a rock, and threw it in with a big splash.

It was a pleasant day, one where it wasn't so hot you broke a sweat just by breathing. A gentle breeze caressed his shins, arms, and face.

He had been watching the police activity around the Devil Tree from afar but with great interest. They had finally loosened their belts on keeping a close watch over Oak Hammock Park and everyone coming in and out of it. This was his only chance to put this new plan into motion.

Travis turned away from the body of water and looked at the forest. It was a sunny day, almost blindingly so, but he knew that evil still existed in the light. Unbeknownst to most people, it roamed the streets during the day as well as under the cover of darkness. Most thought it waited until night to strike and only had power then. That wasn't true. Of course the darkness added to the sense of dread, added another level of fear, but the power it possessed could be used in the light all the same. The tree stood in the daytime, didn't it?

With the idea that this location, this tree, was no longer a viable spot to hold meetings and give sacrifice to his master, he started on the path that took him to the Devil Tree. There were no nerves, no sense of worry—just the sense of needing to get something done.

Travis looked in awe at the ancient mammoth: the gnarled limbs, the Spanish moss, the hidden demon that leapt from branch to branch, and of course the tainted grounds that were forever stained with the evil of Schaeffer and the blood of so many victims.

The group of followers that looked to continue his evil genius had been severely torn apart by the authorities. Travis shrugged. There would always be more. The tree created that allure.

Looking back on the trail, he saw that he was alone. Travis sighed. He felt at home and didn't want to leave, but he knew he must.

When he first arrived in the park there was only one family playing at the playground. There was a young mother, father, and two little kids. Twins maybe. He exchanged pleasantries with them, offering them a warm smile and a shy greeting that would give them no indication of who he was or why he was there.

He peeled a piece of bark off the tree. He inspected it and then put it in his mouth and chewed it and swallowed it. The tree would forever be within him.

He jumped up and wrapped his arms around a low branch. He swung his legs up and maneuvered himself so that he straddled the branch. He could see the marks from the ropes that had scarred the tree. Removing a large Ziploc bag from his pocket, he unzipped it and opened it up. He started picking acorns and loading them into the bag.

He planned on collecting as many as a hundred. Then he would take the evil seeds from the Devil Tree and plant its children elsewhere. He had many locations in mind and couldn't wait to see the young trees grow into something like their mother.

This would give him plenty of places to leave sacrifices and grow his army. He couldn't wait to share his brilliant plan with his followers.

When I returned to the Devil Tree approximately 30 days after I wrote the first book, I wanted a picture that showed you the sheer size of this ancient oak.

Here is the sign for the back entrance into Oak Hammock Park. There's a dilapidated meager fence behind the sign that's overgrown with underbrush and trees.

What remains here is the corner of a structure that once stood not too far away from the Devil Tree. The cinderblock wall, stained with moss and overtaken by the forest is believed to have been from the early 1920s from a structure that served as a boys club. Named differently back then because boys clubs did not exist, these walls are set just beyond the Devil Tree, hiding in plain sight.

Here is a clear shot of another wall that had crumbled over time or had
given in to vandals. Some of these walls stretch as long as ten to twenty
feet, and back in the day there were multiple dwellings.

The age-ravaged corner is still sturdy after all these years. It is believed
that a larger portion of these structures stood during the Schaefer murders. It is believed that he used them as cover and possibly a way to keep
his victims captive before taking them over to the Devil Tree.

This is probably one of the more interesting pictures of the ruins. Straight down the somewhat overgrown path, the foliage opens up and brings you to the Devil Tree. The mangled metal you see beyond the wall frames is the remnants of the corrugated rooftops. Rust shows it has been sitting in the ruins for quite some time, but there is evidence that human interaction has scattered the pieces and even bent them.

Here is a perfect shot of the crumbled walls and how the forest has taken over the area in and around them. To the right, hidden well within the brush (not pictured) is a wooden post and chicken wire fence that is bent over. The rot on the wood is consistent with the moss and corrosion of the corrugated scraps of metal. The oddest rumor I have heard about the ruins beyond the Devil Tree is that there is a hidden trap door to an underground room. I searched for hours and could find no such evidence. Please keep in mind I go in with a very skeptical eye and I'm a show-me type person. Although I felt no fear by the Devil Tree or within the ruins, I did feel there there is something afoul there. It is hard to explain, and I hope as I continue my investigation into the legend my feelings will become more clear.